The Dream Influencer

Andrew Thurlow

Andrew Thurlow

Introduction

When memories become maps, dreams become the only way home.

Eugene and Will believed freedom lay ahead, yet paradise proved only a passing crossroads. Will drifts toward Leyla, a woman chasing the ghost of a dream, as Eugene's creation becomes her fragile salvation.

Reunited at last, Eugene and Paige descend once more into the shifting dreamscape, searching for the boy who whispers of a brighter tomorrow.

In the haunting finale of the Dream Vision Trilogy, time and memory fold in on themselves, and the veil between past, future, and fantasy dissolves one final time.

If you see yourself on the page, its the best version of you

Also by

Also by this Author

The Colour of God (2023)

The Dream Photographer (2025) – Part One of the Dream Vision Trilogy

The Moment Thief (2025) – Part Two of the Dream Vision Trilogy

Chapter One

Consolidation

Paige sat in her Islington flat, a little dumbfounded.

The train ride home had been such a rollercoaster of mixed emotions. She had laughed, been surprised, gotten angry, become disgusted in herself, terrified at the future, wrapped in a mystical joy and then cried unabashedly.

When she got home the whole wash had left her unsure of what she had just done. Had she said the right words, was she clear enough.

Why did her puppy not follow her home.

After sitting downstairs in the dark for an hour Paige got up and moved to the bathroom. Naked and cold she stood in front of the mirror looking at herself. She had always liked the full length mirror view of herself but for some reason today she was not happy with what she saw. She was short, skinny and gaunt. Her small asian breasts and bony hips were not attractive.

Was that what was wrong?

She immediately discounted that, Eugene was not so superficial.

Had he said he loved her?

She tried to recall the conversation in Amsterdam. It was a muddle in her head, all she could recall involved her blurting out a bunch of nonsense that was very unimportant to what she wanted to get out of the conversation. Paige stood for a while longer trying to recollect when she got to the important bit, but she couldn't.

"I love you Eugene. I want us to be together."

Did she say those words?

She remembered rehearsing them again and again on the train, but did she deliver.

She felt very prepared during the trip from London and she had even rehearsed it over and over on the walk from the station to the De Witt but she remembered getting quite flustered when he arrived. Even more so when he was finally standing there in front of her again.

Maybe what I said wasn't clear.

Then he had to go. He had to go on the run! Never failing to surprise, that was Eugene.

She had no doubt he knew what he was doing and as much as she didn't want to know, she knew he was a complex character. He had a very strong moral compass, but it didn't always point true north and he had never been one to follow all the rules to the letter. A lot of the other people around her followed the rules, were educated, but tended to use the little corner of knowledge they possessed to either further their own needs or repress others. Paige's world was all about traditional and respect, Eugene was all about action and discovery. If he didn't know, he found out and he saw the journey of discovery as something that should be shared.

She had hugged him. She recalled that part. He had hugged her back, which felt so good.

Eugene was a very tactile man, it was something she really like about him. It wasn't a creepy touching, if anything he was initially reserved. As time progressed between them he had always had the ability to touch her just in the right place at the right time. Paige took a moment to fold herself in the memories of being wrapped in his arms again. They weren't chiselled arms, alabaster gym arms, they had character, they had blemishes and flaws, moles and scars, they were strong like a well told story. The warmth of that was snatched away as she was reminded she hadn't put on any central heating and it was bitingly cold.

Moving to the shower and turning on the tap Paige remembered what he had said.

"Nothing in the world is more important to me than you."

But she didn't reply.

Disappointed with herself she remember his last words. "There is so much more I need to say. So much I need to hear. But right now I need to go."

She didn't say it.

"You are such a dumb-ass Paige," she chided herself emphatically.

The water finally reached a temperature somewhere above freezing and she ventured into the streaming jets of water. The warmth rose to match that of her body and finally she could relax and let the day wash away.

International rail journeys were generally quite civilised, this one wasn't especially over crowded, travelling either way. Unfortunately from Kings Cross to the Angel was a single tube stop and it was full of the great unwashed in transit to who knows where, so on arriving home it was all she could smell.

She added some rose jam shower gel and breathed in the tangy aromas of flowers and citrus. That was a good start. Paige often found it took more than a single fragrance to remove the bouquet of the underground.

She took her time in the shower, maybe it was in an effort to cleanse the stupid that she felt enveloped her or maybe just a way to block out the world for a while. The joy of being disconnected was something that was lost, until moments like this.

"We need to keep talking," that's what he said.

No, wait. He said "We need to keep talking, beautiful." Paige smiled emphatically feeling additionally special at the addition of that word.

He had once explained why he called her beautiful. Like all women she wanted to believe it was because she was pretty. Pretty could be considered a synonym of beautiful. Pleasing or attractive in a graceful or delicate way, but that's not the way Eugene explained it. He told her he hadn't called any other woman beautiful before and won't again. Not because none of them had been pretty but because beauty is more than just an appreciation of visual stimulation,

3

beauty is a personal concoction of elegance, grace, allure, charm, statue and radiance. In his eyes, she was that mix. Not perfect, because beauty is never perfect.

Eugene always had a way of making her think. Sometimes when they were face to face and he said things like that. She would just get lost in his green eyes and enjoy to the tone of his warm voice, that deep rumbling hum that shook her to her primal core. When she thought back on those words, she would wonder if what he said was really what he meant. Especially when that conversation was digital she would read his words over and over and analyse them. In her most vulnerable of moments she would wonder.

"Did he say, I wasn't perfect."

Later she would ask him and he would reassure her in more conventional terms. To an extent that was his confirmation. He would laugh and say it was his testimony.

The warmth of the shower and the memory of his voice melted Paige into the steam of the shower for a lingering moment.

She wanted to feel his arms around her again. With his arms around her the rest of the world didn't matter.

***

Eugene knew her thoughts would be consuming Paige.

She would say 'they can all go to hell', but then when they were in place, bleating from their fiery cages her guilt would rise. At first it would just be a small whisper in her quiet moments, slowly that whmiper would grow to become chatter that would then exponentially escalate to a deafening siren.

Her family, in particular, seemed to know which levers to pull, a lot of it was guilt, some of it was fear, some of it was cultural conformity and convention. Things that had been ingrained in her psyche since birth. Her pillars. They were professionals at seeking out results that were beneficial to them and even though he never met them, he figured that was not him.

After setting up at the first campsite he had messaged her to say he was thinking about her. Nothing complicated, no location, no direction, just that simple message. His complex encrypted messaging system didn't use anything that could be traced or tracked. His roaming satellite modem was not even purchased in Europe and was not in his name.

When he got to the second campsite and there was no reply, he was a little disappointed but he knew what Paige's response regime was. It was erratic, followed by immersive. Sort of an all or nothing approach. Still nothing when he got to Bulgaria, nothing in Georgia and only when he got to Azerbaijan did he finally get something and in true Paige fashion it was all.

She went over the top, said she would follow him anywhere and be there for him.

Eugene was not falling for that.

"Sorry beautiful, you need to wait until I am settled, you need to converse with your family. You need to explain to your friends, somehow you need to face your demons." He had thought carefully through how to do this right, if he ever got a second chance, he had to make it work.

The Villa, on the outskirts of Baku, had a large private wing that Eugene had taken up residence in. Self contained with kitchen, en-suite bathroom, lounge, large bedroom and study. At first Will was a little overwhelmed by the size of the Villa but he soon settled in. With Eugene taking up the key unit that left pretty much the rest of the place to Will. The showpiece was the large entertaining area that stretched its glory onto a huge balcony which overlooked the sea.

Eugene found Will stretched out on the outdoor lounge. He looked like he had settled in well given the short time they had been in Baku.

"Feeling at home?" Eugene quipped.

"Indeedy I am," Will replied, a big smile brewing under his designer sunglasses.

"Thought we would be lying low, hiding out or something," Will laughed.

"We are," Eugene replied sternly. "Just because we are hiding out doesn't mean we have to suffer."

"That fridge looks absolutely golden," Will cried. "I honestly had no idea they made that many beers in Azerbaijan, aren't they Muslim or something?"

"They are," Eugene smiled an open grin. "Considered the most secular of all Muslim countries. As long as we don't throw it in their faces, we will be fine. The guy that set all this up for me will come back in a few days to restock the fridges, if you want anything else, let me know and he will get it."

Will held up both thumbs in a universal sign of approval with a cheesy grin on his face for confirmation.

"In the mean time can you try and stay close by and be low key, for my sake." Eugene knew that no amount of cajoling would change Will, he was who he was, but he could only try.

"I'm going to soak up some sun while it's still out." Will shouted diving head first into the infinity pool that straddled the balcony.

"Oh chilly," He shrieked as he surfaced toward the middle of the pool. "Thought I would go for a walk along the beach a bit later, promise I'll wear my hat and sunnies. Beer at 5pm."

Eugene turned his upper body and popped up a single thumb to signify that he liked the sound of that.

It was reaching mid morning so that gave Eugene long enough time to set everything up and prioritise some of the tasks he had set himself to achieve here. First and foremost was to change the vocal skin on Daaisi. Wouldn't want Paige turning up and hearing anything that might be a little tricky to explain. There was really no limit to the choices he had, Daaisi could take any vocal tone, replicate it and replay it. The audio application he had developed would research, capture or adapt what it didn't know. Maybe though, it was time Daaisi developed a unique speech pattern.

Now that would be a challenge.

Instead of a single voice pattern to copy he could develop a series of parameters and allow Daaisi to formulate the vocal strings based on similar sound waves. Eugene spent about two hours modifying the parameter set and turned Daaisi loose to become acquainted. He took a moment to make himself a coffee and returned.

"Vocal pattern system check."

"Vocal Systems operating within declared parameters." The voice was very generic, neither male nor female, it was English but not British and also not

American. It had hints of clipped English the sort you find in Ireland or Australia or the West Indies but it also seemed to contain no accent. Or was it a mixture of all of them.

"Intriguing," Eugene said. "Was code modified to reach this outcome?" he asked.

"Currently using Daaisi vocal skin 1.03.251."

Eugene was a little surprised and ran some commands on his device to check.

"Seven hundred and eighty changes while I made coffee," he sighed.

"The outcome to achieve was familiarisation but during the process I determined some improvements in inflection, consistency and understand-ability." Daaisi enunciated.

"Of course you did," Eugene smiled. "I think it's perfect. Were systems integration with the Villa successful?"

"Partial integration is complete. All camera's, automated locks and sensors can now be controlled remotely."

With that out of the way Eugene turned his attention back to the dream interceptor. Somehow he needed to find the problem the unit was causing. The last readings from Adrie were very complete, she had a build up of blood which had left some very strong clues in the diagnostic logs of the unit. The diagnostics seemed to correlate with Adrie's change to REM sleep. Eugene meticulously checked through the code that recorded brain patterns at that time.

"Correlate appearances of anomalous dream totems with an increase in power amplification within sixty seconds of the change to REM sleep in all instances."

"Ninety six percent of all dream totem appearances had an increase in power amplification." Daaisi replied.

"Did the other four percent of dream totem appearances show increased amplification at other times?" Eugene chose his words carefully.

"Yes."

"How many instances is that and at what time interval."

"That is two instances at time intervals sixty one and sixty three seconds."
Eugene just couldn't seem to get the nuances of standard deviation right.

"So, that should be one hundred percent of the time if we include a five percent
standard deviation," he added.

He had located the amplifier in the centre of the flexible circuit board which was
housed very centrally in the dream interceptor.

"Correlate the location of the amplifier in relation to key blood vessels in the
brain. Particularly those around the mid cortex."

"That is a one hundred percent correlation," Daaisi replied.

Eugene made some changes to his schematic. Modifying the strength of the
amplifiers and placing them further to the extremity of the unit.

"Run some diagnostics on board design 127.87.c54. Use data from all known
dream totem appearances to determine the likely effect of amplification changes
on subjects." Eugene requested forcefully.

"Diagnostics will require seven hours using all available processing." Daaisi used
an easy tone to advise the detail.

"Until tomorrow then," Eugene uttered as he got up from his chair and headed
for the door.

The comment was rhetorical and while Daaisi had a large selection of
questions used to produce an effect or to make a statement, rather than
to elicit information, and recognised this as such, the current programming
encouraged silence.

Eugene had used his full quota of time and so he wandered out of his private
area to the kitchen grabbing an apple from the fridge on the way. The view
from the kitchen window was spectacular, the sky had flourished into a
cerulean spectacular and was beginning to transform into a twilight that would
undoubtedly showcase the beauty of Baku's beaches. The fading light had
started to introduce a pale dusty cantaloupe hue and he expected it would catch
fire into bright hot swirls of deep oranges and fiery reds before finally burning
into a crescendo. No doubt that would linger as a tortuous cry until the deep
blues and greys swallowed the day and gave rise to the night's blackness.

"We might need to make that something stronger," said Will from a nook he had perched himself in over looking the pool and the Caspian Sea.

"Nice spot," Eugene commented. He had been quite lost in his thoughts but returned quickly.

"As ordered I have been keeping a low profile," Will smiled.

"Doing it tough," Eugene joked.

"Taking one for the team." Will dropped down from the ledge moving to the outside BBQ area. Without great difficulty or any particular talent he had foreseen this moment and had strategically relocated several of the beers from the inside fridge to this area. He randomly removed two of the same name and handed one to Eugene.

Eugene held up his apple in silent protest.

"Shall I get you a Cider sir." Will quipped draining a significant portion of his first beer, a crisp pacific ale.

Eugene took another bite and moved closer to the BBQ area putting the remainder of the apple in the bin. He matched Will's initial swig and took a seat at the outdoor table.

"This could be hard to get used to," Will said.

"I am amazed we got here without any issues," Eugene replied.

'Well," Will added. "You had the magic grease and a few good contacts." He made the universal sign for money followed by a little explosion with the fingers on his right hand.

Eugene allowed himself a smile. He knew it wasn't over. Daaisi had been scanning Interpol channels looking for any word, and so far there was none. They moved slow, but it would come. Daaisi had also gained access to the hospital records and was tracking Adrie's progress. She remained in a coma, alive and physically quite well. The only issue was the stroke she had suffered. Eugene knew he wouldn't be the only one to check on Lem's autopsy record and realise that it was a stroke in the same area of the brain.

Paradise this was, but trouble would come.

***

The day had started slowly for Wim as many of them did.

Most days were long and slow, he would often use the phrase 'The wheels of justice turn slow' and it was pretty close to the mark. Wim often pondered that the general slowness of the job is what called so many officers to task when something genuinely exciting actually turned up. There always seemed to be complaints of under staffing and excessive over time, but when a murder or gangland killing was reported, there seemed to be an endless stream of officers on hand. Many were not dispatched and many were not actually required but, in many of these cases, there seemed to be an overwhelming urge to show force after the fact.

Monday had started as a less than interesting day, again. Wim had been tidying up a myriad of things that were placed on his desk, both when he was and when he wasn't sitting at it, until he was redirected.

Since the redirection he had waited patiently in his car for the breach team to complete their work. Just like he had waited patiently for the warrant to come through and almost waited patiently for surveillance to complete. He had taken only one shift with Officer Barend, as part of the surveillance team. He didn't need to be on this case but he wanted to take down the shifty guy. He was sure that guy was behind this, not Eugene Baltes.

The breach was fast. Second strike was on the lock in the front which did not withstand the force unlike the main glass window which appeared to be ballistic glass.

"Who were these people?" he had thought to himself.

The strike team had entered and cleared the building. Wim didn't wait long, as soon as the first floor was clear, he had followed.

"A.I." He shouted nonspecifically to the room.

The nothingness replied.

"I am Detective Wim Hummel, we have legal forced entry and search warrants." Wim had held the warrants above his head.

Still more nothing.

A large heavy set officer, clad in body armour, helmet and equipped with shotgun broke the silence and marched forcefully towards Wim taking the hallway in a few strides

"Breach complete." He growled.

"Anyone here?" Wim had replied in a similar gruff voice, not his usual voice, he felt the need to match the intensity of the breach officer.

"Empty." The officer had replied. Wim could see the disappointment from the dip in his shoulders.

"OK, Thank you."

"The place is yours detective. My team will be outside for another hour before we return to base."

Wim didn't make any follow up statements, he knew the procedure.

He had been looking around the servery and had found very little of interest. His uncle had run a bakery and had a front room very similar to this one. If he was honest, in his opinion, his uncle could open up and sell bread tomorrow. Moving down the hall towards the kitchen he had admired the workmanship. The place was expertly renovated, with style and functionality. The kitchen was a mass of modern storage and bench space, dominated by a large red coffee machine.

Wim had been trying to find information on the Internet about the "Marketing Research" done here. The information seemed to be very sparse, he suspected most of it had been recently removed. He had found a small amount in a cache on Reddit. Something about being a 'Dream Photographer', Wim had thought it was financial research.

The two day rooms left no clue for him. It was all very sterile. There was no document storage, just the one desk in a small office and no accommodation at all. Unsure of what he should be looking for, Wim had paced back to the servery and out the front door. Walking the perimeter he made some mental notes on the buildings windows and general dimensions before returning inside. First stop, the garage, there had been room for another vehicle. The Audi that had remained was nice, not flashy, just comfortable. There were large racks for storage but most of it was empty.

"There was another car," Wim had said to no-one in particular.

"Something you need detective?" A junior officer was standing in the hall and heard Wim talking.

"Did we check the number of cars registered to this address?"

"I will check with the detective." The officer had said as he turned and moved down the hall.

"I will be upstairs," Wim called out heading for the elevator.

The upstairs storage rooms were some high tech stuff. They appeared to be digitally controlled, the breach team had forced one and found it empty. Wim would need to wait for his own tech team to arrive to sweep the place, forcing things was not going to get them any answers. He walked to where the external window should have been, but there was wall. He tapped the wall and got a dull thud, maybe he would need to check better outside. Wim wasn't one to doubt himself but he decided it wouldn't hurt to go outside and take some better notes. He started looking at the storage room on the first floor where the window was. There should have been the same size again behind that wall, maybe even another room.

Wim had taken some notes on the structure while outside including the second floor and had then returned to the storage area. This time he took with him the breach Sargent who seemed very happy when asked to punch a hole through the wall. When the hole showed a work area and a second clandestine elevator to the second floor he knew things were not as they seemed. When the tech team turned up he had already got a better idea of how the building was structured. Not that it helped as he still had no idea what they did here. There were no signs of anything personal, no photographs, no clothing, nothing. At first Wim thought it had been stripped, but the junior detectives all thought perhaps it had never been used. There was significant dust in the clandestine areas, consistent with not being used for at least a few months.

The tech team came, spent three days combing the building, and went. They found most of the code for the operation of the building intact, cameras, elevators, even the small robots that cleaned and seemed to move things around. They noted however that there was no data, no employee data, no client data and no personal data.

Even more surprising was the forensic team's report. No fingerprints, anywhere. Not in the private quarters, not in the bathrooms, not in the kitchen. The place had been meticulously cleaned. They did find some hair but this would be useless unless they could match it, which they could not.

Wim was frustrated. They had almost nothing.

Back at the station he and the team went through what they did have. A company structure, which, according to his financial forensic team was complicated. The accounts seemed to have transactions coming in and going out from many international companies. Not many in Europe, some in the US, some as far away as New Zealand. The company was profitable, up to date on its taxes and very clean. Wim would suspect it was almost too clean. He quickly received authority to investigate and if necessary to freeze all accounts. Maybe this would help him determine where these people had gone. Wherever it was, they had not gone in a hurry and they had covered their tracks well.

He found the other car registered to the address was a Range Rover, top of the line.

"There is no way that this building and this top of the line Range Rover were purchased from these finances." Wim reiterated to the forensic accountant that sat across from him in the case meeting. "So we need to know where the money came from." His frustration was clear for all to see.

"The car was purchased seven years ago as part of a business loan that shows regular interest payments, followed by a final payoff last year." The accountant was trying valiantly to play catch up with Wim's hypothetical statements. "The building was part of the stated seed funding from initial investment."

"So where did that come from." Wim was trying to stay calm.

"Initial investment was from a Cayman Islands account." The accountant looked like he had been drinking over lunch and stammered slightly. "All the appropriate taxes were paid, all the official permits were sought and granted."

"The business is just one guy or maybe two, and generates five million Euros annually. How is this possible? Legally?" Wim added a slap on the table to give the last words gravitas.

"Yes Detective Hummel. We understand your frustration." The captain had sat in on this case meeting. Less because he had any interest but more because this strange case was now taking a significant amount of resources he had promised to dedicate to the gangland problems that plagued Rotterdam. "We are investigating a murder case, not looking for international conspiracy."

"I need to use this detail to track where this fugitive has gone," Wim pleaded.

"We have locked his, or their finances and we are monitoring accounts and identities." The captain had not attended any long lunch and did not drink during the day, so was very alert. He was also more attuned to procedure than emotion which is probably why he was captain and Wim was not. "He or they will be picked up eventually."

"But we have the best chance picking them up on a hot trail, a cold trail might take years. These are very clever individuals. We should be able to pull some Autobahn license recognition with minimal effort. We have him in Hilversum we know he went East."

"I agree." the captain was not disagreeing with the last statement. "These are clever criminals, but I need you to catch more less clever individuals rather than spend most of your time and the time of forensic investigators and half the station on this one case."

"Let's allow time to do some work for us here," the captain sighed.

***

Eugene had accumulated significant money over the five years since he sold his software business, paid his taxes and funnelled the money through the Cayman's to invest in the setup in Rotterdam.

But whatever was being unravelled now was just the screen he had created to hide his true actual source of income, which was cryptocurrency. His skill with business systems had allowed him to create an untranslatable myriad of transactions and accounts spread across borders, languages and jurisdictions which would mean he knew he had a least a year or two before anyone could catch up with where the money actually was.

It hurt a little as he watched the breach team destroy the bakery. He did like the place and he loved Rotterdam. He took note as they froze his accounts. To try to add to the confusion he initiated a transaction from an account he held in Morocco, it might work to put them off the very, very thin trail he had left.

In the meantime he closed some other business accounts he had in Europe. Spanish, Lithuanian and Romanian accounts could all give up more pieces of the European puzzle he had created and closing them now might just provide the gap needed when, or if, they were eventually investigated.

He had also been thinking about the Range Rover. Any link may give him away, so he sent off a message to his agent that he wanted the car chopped up and sold with a new car leased with some paperwork in another name, as soon as possible. He was glad he had changed license plates as they left Hilversum, it was a good move that he had Will to thank for.

Chapter Two

Way more trouble than it's worth

The sunshine was glorious, buoyantly and exuberantly spreading it rays eastward as it embraced the sprawling coastline.

At Eugene's request, Will had spent the first two weeks squirrelled away in the Villa. It was not a tough ask. The Villa was a marvellous playground, the pool was sublime and there was a fully equipped gym, spa and sauna. Will was not a health nut, but it helped him to pass the time. Complimenting that, the library had a pretty complete array of actual hardcover books and Eugene had pointed him at his endless supply of e-books, audio books, documentaries, movies and TV series.

So Will saw it less about being locked up and more about Will being distracted.

The beer helped.

As things seemed to be going well, Will knew he wouldn't be locked up for long. Eugene had given his blessing for Will to walk on the beach and explore the coastline a little. He had asked nicely for Will to try and keep a low profile and stay out of any local business. Eugene must have known Will would head straight for the nearest bar but he had furnished Will with some walking around money in the hope Will would keep clear of trouble.

Seemed like a big ask to Will, but he would try. He wanted to remind Eugene that no-one was looking for him, or knew who he was, but he thought better of that argument.

After two weeks in the Villa, his first walk on the beach had gone without incident. The second, Eugene came with him, so that was also all clear.

On the third, the day was just too striking to be cooped up inside. Will wandered slowly through the golden sand amazed at the beach-line's mix of Villa's, hotels, houses and mansions. He saw a few people walking on the beach, ambling listlessly with their dogs or just enjoying the relative serenity of the evenings.

As time progressed, Will started taking a full uninterrupted walk up the beach in the mornings and then a whistle stop walk, taking in a few bars at a time, along the beach strip on each afternoon.

He tried hard to keep to himself but Will was not the kind of guy that goes unnoticed and on such a visit to one of the sprawling hotel bars he was approached by Leyla.

Leyla was not Will's usual type of lady. She was a little older, very sophisticated, intelligent and refined. Will had seen her walking on the beach in the afternoons and she had seen him in another smaller bar further up the beach a few days earlier.

The two talked for a few hours the first time, they danced and played with words around each other, talked without meaning, laughed without understanding and tip toed around the core subjects of life by discussing trivialities. Based on a common interest in each other, they planned to meet up again the following day for coffee.

Later that night Leyla called him and the two met in the front cabana of her Villa. Will was far too distracted by Leyla to think about how big the structure behind the cabana might be or who lived there. Perhaps if he had bothered to check this out before he proceeded he might have thought twice. Then again he probably wouldn't. Consequence was never his thing.

He thought Leyla might have been swayed before by many a good looking, smooth talking man and tonight would be no different. The truth is she seemed to enjoy making love, she made love physically, passionately.

Will held her in a bit of a trance for an hour before she became lost in her first orgasm, then another hour before the second wave shook her body. By the time Will positioned himself to end this first encounter they were both drained of all energy and lost to the moment.

"Where did you come from dear," she groaned as Will got up from the bed and dressed.

"Most recently Europe but I come from a land down under," Will smiled.

"You did," Leyla smiled.

"Are you in town for a while?" she asked pleadingly.

"Sure hope so," he grinned, stooping to kiss her before heading for the bathroom.

"I'll just be five."

Will returned partially clothed and looking to complete his ensemble and make an exit.

"Are you on a curfew?" she asked a little confused at Will's sudden need to leave.

"I am not," Will said quietly. "There is a guy in the garden with a torch and in my experience this doesn't end well for me."

"It's just the security guard," Leyla smiled. "He patrols, but he wont bother us in here, he knows better."

"Security guard looked a lot like police to me." Will said looking over his shoulder slightly.

"Yes," she said, "about that." Leyla paused and sighed. "My husband is the chief of police here in Baku."

"Chief!" Will breathed out. "Never by halves Wilberforce," he muttered to himself. "Then I really should be going," he smiled.

"Oh darling, just one kiss and a small hug. Ten minutes at most. No-one will disturb us, really you must wait for him to make his way around the Cabana before you leave now or he will be alerted." She smiled seductively.

Will acquiesced magnanimously. He found himself particularly attracted to Leyla, so it wasn't a that much of a struggle.

She was petite but not short, slim but not skinny, bronzed but not dark, pretty but not stunning and mostly she was enchanting. He saw her as without boundaries, pretty much like he saw himself. Many people fit into boxes, they choose lives that suit those boxes or the boxes choose them based on their passive attitudes to conflict. Will hadn't determined the box that Leyla inhabited yet and he liked that.

Will was not a box man.

In the two hours of conversation and the associated thirty minutes of texting the subject of partners had not come up. Will didn't have one so maybe he just assumed that was the way it was. He doubted it would have mattered if he had known and now he really only cared if it caused conflict.

***

Eugene waited for the connection protocol to complete. The days of modem handshake noises were gone but the application he had modified to use had a similar rhythmic progression. The audio and video made a connection at exactly the same time, and there she was beaming at him.

"Hello Eugene." Paige's smile was exactly the glowing brightness he was waiting for.

"Hello Beautiful," he grinned.

"How are you?" She added "Am I allowed to ask where you are?" She was still smiling but a glimpse of concern grasped the corner of her eyes.

"I'm good. On the edge of Europe but very much in civilisation, maybe better if you don't know for now."

"Fair enough," she returned to her full beaming smile.

"I need to," Paige stopped mid sentence. Eugene waited, she seemed to be struggling. "I just need to say." She stopped again.

Eugene started to become a little nervous. "I love you Eugene. I want us to be together." She burst out, starting to cry a little.

"Yes beautiful, I love you too. It will happen, we just need to be patient," Eugene replied remaining calm.

"I meant to say it in Amsterdam, but I got distracted when you hugged me," she said sobbing.

Eugene smiled again. Hugs can do that. Not just his hugs, any hugs. Eugene watched as she dried her tears.

"I have so much to tell you. How long can we talk for?"

Eugene had thought through that exact point. The encrypted communications reset its path every minute, he figured the answer was that there was no limit. However, knowing Paige he thought it might be easier to keep to conversation limited.

"We need to keep this under ten minutes," he said. "But I can call you again tomorrow if you can make time, and every day." Eugene knew smaller conversations would be better while they were apart. Hopefully it would stop her getting overly emotional, although that premise seemed to be failing him now.

"Tell me," he confirmed quickly.

"Well I listened Eugene. I took what you said in Amsterdam to heart. I am going to start by leaving my job. The whole place has degraded remarkably since the main director died recently. I found some ads for part time remote stuff, perfect for me. It will give me time during the day to do what I like but provide enough contact that I don't lose touch. I haven't applied yet. What do you think?"

"That sounds great," Eugene was very encouraging of Paige's career. Whenever she didn't work she got so distracted and upset by unimportant things.

"Work is good to help you keep to a routine but I think doing the things you love is important too. Have you done any painting lately?" Eugene asked.

"Thanks. I know it's not much, but I made bigger steps. I just haven't found the right moment for painting, but I will try. I sat down with my Mum and Dad and my sister. They are so difficult to crack but I told them I was leaving London and going to do some travel. I think they pretty much see me as a little bit crazy and when I said I didn't know where to, they offered to take me on holidays." Paige laughed, "but I stayed strong and convinced them to let me go it alone."

"Well, that's a start I suppose," Eugene grinned a little.

"I am having dinner with a few friends tomorrow night." Paige stopped for a moment. "I don't think I will have any trouble with them but give me a few more days to work myself out, clean up my stuff." Paige looked into the camera pleadingly.

"Yes okay," Eugene didn't want her to rush. Rushing her would have a bad affect for the future and he would regret that later.

"Just one thing," she looked a little perplexed. "About what you said in Amsterdam."

"Sure," Eugene said confidently. "Fire away."

"Well you said if anyone contacted me, that I should deny all knowledge. I haven't said anything about you to my family and I won't to my friends but I am a little confused. Why are you on the run?" Paige made a face that could only be described as screwed up.

Eugene held back a laugh. He knew this was important, it wasn't that she asked, it was the way Paige had said it.

"You know those intense dreams I got, which then moved to the ones you got." He explained.

"Yes," she said. "I'm still getting them."

"Really," he was a bit taken aback by that answer but stayed on track. "Well, looks like they were caused by a fault with the dream interceptor."

"A fault." she said.

"Yes," Eugene explained. "Some of the electronics were causing blood to flow where it shouldn't and that meant our brains were a little overloaded and the dreams were just in reaction to that. I saw it in a number of my other subjects, particularly the ones that returned multiple times, ones I tried to get information from."

"Right, and one died." Paige said looking even more puzzled.

"Yes," Eugene admitted. "I didn't know what to do so I made the problem go away. Then another test subject had a stroke and that was something I couldn't hide. I haven't been charged with anything yet but I didn't want to put myself in the firing line. Once they had me I would suggest they wouldn't let me go, but now I can claim plausible deniability, if they ever catch up with me."

"Right," said Paige. "So what's my part?"

"Well, no-one else has ever been registered at the dream bakery, except you." Eugene knew this was not going to go down well. "So there is an off chance they might ask you some questions, because the address and number you gave at the time was the address and number of your London flat."

"Ah yes," she remembered. "That was when those nice border control people visited wasn't it? They seemed okay with everything."

"Yes," he said. "However, they took down your details and would have recorded it somewhere. So when they can't find me, they might just ask you as you are the only other person they have on file."

"Ah!" Paige was going to cry. "So what am I supposed to do?"

Eugene kind of had this worked out.

"Nothing. I think you should just go about things the way you were going to. If they ask you, just say you left a year ago and haven't seen me since. That will check out with whatever they find because it's true. If they don't contact you, and you are ready I will make plans on how to get you here."

"Okay." Paige wasn't sure but went along with it.

"Anyway, times up beautiful. Do you have time tomorrow?" Eugene smiled his best loving smile.

"I will make time." Paige said determined.

"Love you." Eugene said meaningfully.

"Love you too," Paige said blowing him a kiss as the call ended.

Eugene was convinced the plan would be okay if Paige held it together, which was a big ask.

"I wonder what she meant by 'still getting them'" Eugene said out loud.

I will have to ask tomorrow.

***

"The activity in Morocco shows that Eugene Baltes has gone into Africa." the forensic accountant said, being annoying.

"It shows he has triggered some traffic to lead us that way," Wim reiterated. "His web is wide and he is not stupid."

"I am in agreement with Hummel," the captain said adjudicating. "This is not a trail, this is fake."

"I think it shows we are dealing with someone guilty who feels the need to put us off," Wim said directly at the captain.

"Maybe," the captain replied. "We don't know where he is doing that from. He could still be in Europe or could be in New Caledonia by now. I stick by my original plan to wait him out. Did we get anything from Germany on the plates? Or anything from the the dream bakery building?"

"He must have changed plates, we have him leaving Holland then nothing. The residence had only two residents since he purchased it. The second is a British girl who apparently lived on that site a year ago for almost a year."

"What did she have to say?" the captain asked.

"I haven't tried her yet, well outside my jurisdiction and the British never seem that friendly." Wim had been burned too many times before to overstep his mandate.

"I have a contact that will help," the captain said.

***

The results looked clear to Eugene. The changes would minimise the dream interceptors interference on the brain. Daaisi's tests showed that in both Lem and Adrie's situations the changes in the dream interceptor would have not pooled blood in the posterior cingulate cortex. In Adrie's case, with one hundred percent accuracy, her stroke would have been avoided. Lem's case was a little harder to guarantee, with his age and poor health, still the chances were lower remaining around seventy five percent.

This was enough for Eugene. He felt sure he could resume testing, at an appropriate time and place, both of which were not here and not now. While he was reasonably sure that the technology was sound. If, by any chance he was mistaken and another stroke or death occurred he would be back in a situation where he would need to move on and all things being considered he may not be so lucky next time. That was considering he may not have been so lucky the first time as the whole 'get out of town' was done, but not over.

To confirm his suspicions, Paige had received a call that very next day from a constable in Scotland Yard. A simple question.

"Have you seen Eugene Baltes in the last 12 months?"

She said she reacted well and said no. Paige said she told them that they were a couple, but she left, as he was in Rotterdam and she was a Londoner and that was a space they couldn't fill. She said she told them that she tried to move to Rotterdam but it didn't work out and that she missed her family and friends and he didn't want to move so they let it go. She said she told them she had gone for a clean split and hadn't spoken to Eugene since. Paige said the whole conversation lasted ten minutes and ended with the constable asking if she heard from him that she should call them to tell them where he was.

The constable then just seemed to let it go.

Eugene praised Paige highly but then the ten minutes ran out and Eugene had to just promise to talk to her the next day.

***

Will had been enjoying life in Azerbaijan considerably more than he thought he would. It helped that he was living the high life and having regular physical intimacy with a really, really exceptional lover. He lay in his nook contemplating how good things can turn sometimes when Eugene joined him.

"Hey buddy, how goes the tech mogul?" Will quipped.

"I have made some important breakthroughs." Eugene leaned back with a cocked fist and mimed busting through an imaginary wall. "I managed to find the problems with the dream interceptor. All my tests seemed to point to a dream free of potential hazards, present company excepted. I should have new equipment ready by the start of next week and I will start setting up that small front room to run some live tests."

Eugene was still a little unsure of the dreams Will had, but he was sure that they were not normal.

"To be honest I think I am on the verge of something quite amazing," Eugene continued. "I have made a few changes to Daaisi's programming to allow a better cross reference of other dreams. There was already some reference on request but now it all becomes more part of the original render."

"So what does that mean?" Will asked.

"Well," Eugene continued "If you dream of a place and I dream of the same place, Daaisi will make a reference to the similarity of our dreaming and allow there to be closer scrutiny to see if there is a match."

"Right," Will nodded. "Sounds a bit impersonal."

"Yes, possibly," Eugene replied. Not wanting to be drawn in any further Eugene changed the subject.

"So what have you been up to?" he said opening up the floor to hear about Will's exploits. "I notice you have been staying out quite late."

"Yes," Will smiled. "About that."

Eugene nodded and smiled. "You are a quick mover."

"Yes," Will didn't smile back. "Leyla lives a few mansions up that way along the beach, so nice and easy to get to. Nothing much else to report, I think I have visited all the bars within walking distance, not one of them was really worth waxing lyrical about. I would strongly suggest we stay around here and drink the beer in the fridge, unless you want a change of scenery." Will had moved to the fridge and extracted two cold IPAs, handing one to Eugene and taking a large mouthful of his own straight from the bottle.

"I think that sounds like a plan," Eugene replied, in full agreement. He opened his own bottle and proceeded to drink.

"She has a big place and as long as I can continue to dodge her husband and his horde of police security, things will be fine."

Eugene choked slightly but managed to retain his composure "Husband," he said sternly.

"Indeed, not by design." Will explained. "But it is what it is. She said he would be fine with it, but I am a little unsure. It makes me nervous there are police patrolling around all the time but so far so good."

"Police?" Eugene exhaled, the look on his face changed to more a concerned frown than fear.

"Apparently, he is the chief of police," Will smiled.

"Joking right," Eugene retorted.

"I wish," Will struggled to keep his laughter in check. "It seems cool, nothing to do with your problems and if anything there may be a silver lining we don't see yet."

"If we can just not bring her here for the moment, that would be great," Eugene pleaded.

"Obviously," Will's expression returned to the ocean.

"I think I will work out an exit strategy from here," Eugene added. "Any thoughts?" He didn't need Will's help, but thought it was a good thing to keep the spirit of partnership going.

"The next part would be tricky by land so you might be best to look at air travel. Somewhere around India or over India would be best, from there it gets easier to persuade people with the magic dust."

"Yes," Eugene agreed. He had been toying with a driving car but the the thought of travelling through Iran, war torn Afghanistan and anywhere around Pakistan was not exactly appealing.

"My agent said a lot of the dust spread here has been done with good affect. The dream bakery has been compromised but it looks like they didn't find anything significant as most of my cloud infrastructure remains untouched, the just got the bits I left poking out." Eugene smiled and finished the beer, signalling to Will that another was in order. Fetching two, he handed a fresh cold IPA to Will.

"I have had pretty constant contact with Paige, and she will probably join us here, unless things go south and we need to move. She got contact from the police in London and seems to have deflected any suspicion away."

"All right" Will smiled a big grin and got up to pat Eugene on the back.

"I have a pass tonight so we should nail a few more of these," Will encouraged.

Eugene was happy that the friends had some time together and raised his bottle to touch the tip of Will's.

Chapter Three

Shared

"So my dinner was good." Paige had made a list to try and keep things Eugene needed to know as key points of the conversation. The ten minutes restriction very much deprived her of her usual conversational method which was ebb and flow, read and retort. Eugene was very pleased to hear that she hadn't been procrastinating and had in fact been active in sorting out her life.

"That's great to hear," he replied with an air of congratulations in his voice.

"Yes, my friends are supportive of any move I make. They agreed that this time we would do a better job to keep in contact when I go, so I don't miss them so much."

"That sound like a great plan beautiful." Eugene smiled. He had put a filter on his camera so hopefully that smile didn't show up the crow's feet forming around his eyes. Not that he felt Paige needed that superficial reinforcement, just something he did because he could.

"I haven't had any further contact from the police," she smiled. "Looks like you are off and away."

"Yes," Eugene confirmed. "I think we can look to what we do next, if you are ready for that."

"I am!" she shreiked with a mousy tone. "What did you have in mind?"

"Well," he said calmly. "When I left Holland, I did so with a school friend of mine from Australia, who was visiting at the time. His name is Will. We are in a large villa on the Caspian Sea, certainly large enough that if you came too and took a separate guest area, we still wouldn't even fill half of the place. It fronts onto the beach but has a large pool, gym and ... "

"You don't need to sell it to me Eugene. I'm not coming for the real estate." Paige said laughing.

"Yes, quite. Anyway I was thinking if you are okay with it, rather than a direct flight here, which may seem a bit strange, I will book you to first go to Morocco then you can take a second flight here. That way if anyone in London is watching your movements, they wont see your destination."

"Are they watching me?" Paige wanted to turn and look out her kitchen window.

"No beautiful. They're not. Just a precaution."

"Okay," she smiled at him. That was very Eugene.

"Let's leave it another few days, just so you can be sure." He said knowing that she didn't respond to pressure but having to balance her predilection for changing her mind.

Better she changed her mind before, than when she was in Baku.

"If you think its best," she agreed.

"Now while we still have time can I ask about your dreams. You said something that other day that you are still having intense dreams."

"Yes," she said. "The boy. For a while we were in this street, looked like an old style Amercian street with old cars, maybe nineteen hundreds sometime. Then we went back to an island, then a cabin in the woods, the snow. Each time some catastrophe was building and he was warning me. Lately they have subsided a little bit." Paige stopped, thinking what else to add.

"... and the Snake" Eugene interupted.

"Thankfully, nowhere to be seen," she replied.

"So what have you been dreaming lately, if its subsided."

"Let me think."

Paige had kept a journal when she was living in Rotterdam, but Eugene was pretty sure she had let the practice go since returning to London. Hopefully the experience of recording her dreams had put her conscious and subconscious in better contact and had made her ability to recall what she dreamed quite good.

"Last night was a long and winding road through some mountains, when we arrived it was to an old building surrounded by flags. The boy wasn't warning me from this, he was welcoming us."

"Wait" Eugene cut her off abruptly. "I was there?"

"Yes Eugene," she rolled her eyes. "You were in my dreams."

"No," he held up his hand both as an act to stop her from saying anymore but also to steady his own thoughts. "I had that dream too. What about the night before?"

"That was the old cabin in the woods."

Eugene interrupted again. "An island."

"Yes," she said.

"Two out of two. Tell me about the American street."

"Oh that was a few months ago," Paige said. "The night before that was a campsite, somewhere cold."

The time frame of the call was reaching ten minutes. Eugene knew he could continue if he wanted but felt it was better to maintain the pretence.

"Wow," he said. "That is amazing. You were in my dreams to, they sound very similar. I have some research to do."

Paige knew that was Eugene's way. She would hear more about this another time.

"I will keep a better record for you from now on," she smiled.

His heart melted. That smile was an amazing thing. Maybe it was the dimples, maybe the way the rest of her had bound herself around his heart with the smile as just a gentle squeeze, to remind him she was in there.

"We need to go beautiful. Tomorrow at the same time."

"Okay," she said sadly. "I love you Eugene."

The call cut out before he got a chance to say it but he replied with his own love, even though she couldn't hear him.

***

Eugene had been working hard building the new version of the dream interceptor. The work required intense concentration and as his own disciplinarian Eugene insisted on regular breaks. He knew Will had left the complex. He had placed some motion sensors in key choke points around the structure, more for incoming security than to keep tabs on Will but it was in Eugene's nature to want to know where everybody was. The day was cloudy and strong winds forced the cloud ever southeast. The wind came with a Siberian chill that day, unlike most of the other days they had spent in Baku. Eugene could only image that Will had gone to see his lady friend as it was just not beach walking weather.

It was the kind of weather that Eugene liked, so he walked around the pool area inspected the various plants in the garden. More recently he liked to take time away from soldering electronics or programming by concentrating on nothing in particular.

"Hi."

Eugene turned to see someone standing on the beach. She was a medium height, very well presented, slim and the first word he reached for was elegant.

"Hi," he replied graciously.

"How are you?" She asked.

"I'm good. How about you? Bit of a windy day for a walk." Eugene decided idle chit chat was appropriate.

"I'm Leyla," she smiled. "I was looking for Will."

"Yes," Eugene was a little relieved and then surprised.

"Come in. The gate is on the left." Eugene was not so rude as to leave her standing on the beach.

Leyla was dressed in a long flowing dress which was part of an ensemble that included a pantsuit and an under jacket that protected her from the elements perfectly with the option to remove a layer if things brightened up or secure buttons and zips if the weather turned.

"Hello," Eugene said with his hand outstretched. "I am Eugene."

"Yes. Will has told me all about you." Leyla smiled.

"Only the best bits I hope," Eugene laughed.

"Of course," Leyla replied.

"Would you like a coffee?" Eugene asked politely. "I was about to make one."

"Oh thank you, you are too kind. That would be wonderful." Leyla had a beautiful speaking voice, an old world charm with a meticulous grasp on English.

Eugene led her to the outdoor kitchen where he had installed a small espresso machine. He wasn't so trusting or presumptuous as to invite her inside on first meeting, he hoped they could both feel comfortable around the pool even if it was a little chilly after all it was the showpiece of the villa.

"I do like to make all kinds of coffee, do you have a favourite?" He asked politely.

"Oh I love Turkish coffee," she said. "Are you able to make that?"

"Of course" Eugene replied confidently. He had seen a *Cezve* when they first arrived in a cupboard inside. "Would you like sugar with that?" he asked.

"Yes please," Leyla replied.

"I have the *Cezve* inside. I will be just one moment." He motioned towards the kitchen and left her to take a seat.

"Of course," she replied.

Eugene stepped inside and made his way to the kitchen to look for the *Cezve*.

"Daaisi, message to Will, 'Leyla is here at the Villa. I am making her coffee'."

"Message sent, Eugene." Daaisi replied expressively, the new vocal skin giving just the right intonation on confirmation.

Eugene found the distinctive copper pot in the cupboard under the coffee cups and matched it with one of the middle eastern cups that abounded. He also found some *Kurukahveci Mehmet Efendi* coffee which was left over from a previous guest.

Eugene's knowledge of Turkish coffee would be sufficient to make a half decent cup. It was by no means his personal favourite, but he had tried and made so many variations of coffee on his journey through life, he was confident enough to continue.

"I found a very appropriate cup to match," he said returning promptly onto the landing. A light rain started to fall, it was nothing, but the wind made it swirl around the patio area and cascade a million circles on the pool to dance around as the wind distorted them.

"Oh beautiful," Leyla said energetically. Mostly a comment on the cup but then as she looked up she was quite taken by the beauty of nature meeting architecture.

"So Will tells me you are into technology. What sort of technology is that?"

"Well," Eugene replied. "I cover many bases, mostly software development, A.I, some electronics, financial data models, probability. You might say I find projects to work on and have the experience and the drive to make them happen."

"That's wonderful" Leyla complimented. "... and now your project is Dreams."

Eugene was surprised. He placed the Turkish coffee in front of Leyla without a reply and went to make his own espresso.

"Will told me you had a great understanding of dreams and had done some research in Rotterdam," she continued. "What brings you to Baku?"

"Will told you that did he," Eugene said in character. "I have some contacts here at the University that are assisting me," he was nothing if not a good liar when placed on the spot.

"That's nice," Leyla replied. "Dreams certainly are a mystery."

"Yes. I think that is what started me on my journey." Eugene really didn't want to be talking about this.

"So how did you meet Will?" He added moving the subject elsewhere.

"Oh he was bar hopping and I saw him for the third time in two days, so I had to ask what he was doing." she smiled. "The two of us just got talking. It's rare I meet a man who talks the way I do and rarer to find an Australian. We just seem to strike up a relationship from there."

"Yes he's quite the talker," Eugene smiled. "Do I detect in your voice that you have visited Australia?" Eugene added.

"Yes, very good. I completed an arts degree at Melbourne University in my youth. Time well spent." She smiled. "I must admit my interaction with Australians was less than I would have liked. The university seemed full of International Students like me and my mother accompanied me, so there was little chance to mix locally. Maybe I am making up for lost time, now my mother has less grip on my social life."

The rain seemed to dissipate slightly and the wind died significantly. A shroud of quiet descended across the courtyard.

"Melbourne is a nice city." Eugene said "Nicer when I was a kid. It certainly suffers from integration problems these days, probably even more than when you were at University."

"I used to love the inner city around East Melbourne and Carlton," Leyla said dreamily. So many cute cafe's and shops along tree lines streets. Sometime it felt like a bit of a dream to walk around. Certainly a long way from the cramped streets of Old Baku."

"Indeed." Eugene added. "I am sorry I am not sure where Will is. I tried to message him before but he seems to not be replying."

"Yes, maybe I should make a dash while the weather is kind," Leyla said finishing her coffee.

Eugene really didn't want to appear rude but also wasn't keen to have Leyla just sit around waiting for Will who could be five minutes or five hours.

"Very nice to meet you," he added.

"Also you Eugene," she smiled and made her way confidently to the gate and back onto the beach.

***

Will did indeed come back in five hours.

The phone Eugene had given him had run out of charge and he didn't see the need to stress about charging it up so was just enjoying a walk on the beach book-ended by a few beers in a pair of bars.

Will was actually in a very good mood when he returned and was sorry he missed Leyla.

"You shouldn't have told her too much about what's going on here." Eugene was more disappointed than angry,

"Yeah, sorry mate. Slip of the tongue. I will be more careful." Will replied handing Eugene a tropical ale.

"To be honest I just thought we would appear more sus if we keep everything a secret. Whenever I come anywhere new and meet new people if you clam up and don't have a back story they are unlikely to want to engage." Will continued.

Eugene thought for a moment, swilling down a good mouthful of beer.

"You might be right, we didn't really work on that much. I just told Leyla that I was here working with some people at the university." Eugene explained.

"Yeah, that's a great cover. Explains why we came to Baku. Did she buy it?" Will replied.

"Pretty sure she did. The conversation ended there." Eugene shrugged his shoulders. People were not really his thing.

"She might be a good candidate for your re-gigged dream interceptor," Will said flippantly. "Now that its all up to spec."

"She did seem very interested in dreams. If you aren't willing to give it another try, I will need someone new to experiment on." Eugene rubbed his hands like an evil scientist and laughed maniacally.

"Yeah, little too close to home." Will commented.

"I am not sure I am ready to face what's going on in there," he said pointing to his skull. "What you showed me last time was way scarier than I was expecting. I mean I have some pretty bad dreams, things that wake me up in the middle of night in cold sweats, then I go back to sleep. The way you present them, they kind of stay with you and become a little bit more real."

"If you believe the literature," Eugene replied. "They are manifestations of your subconscious reflecting thoughts, feelings and experiences. I wouldn't say they are all you, they are about how other people have treated you as much as how you have treated other people. The results are not immediately apparent and sometimes require further study. I believe I have found there is something more there. It's like we are looking at the outer granite shell of an Egyptian mummy thinking that's the thing. We wont know there is a gold sarcophagus inside without opening it up and having a look."

"It's the opening up that is a bit scary, especially if you go beyond the gold sarcophagus," Will said. "I have had a peek in my own box in my own time and I am quite happy for that box the remain closed for the time being."

"Gotcha," Eugene said pointing two index fingers at Will.

"Maybe Leyla will make a good test. You should invite her over for a coffee, don't offer anything yet, let me talk to her first," Eugene said.

"okey dokey," Will replied getting up from the table and moving inside to charge his phone.

***

The copper pot was a curiosity to Eugene.

It was a coffee brewing method that extracted a product that looked, smelled and tasted stronger than the more complicated pressure extraction of espresso machines, but wasn't. It was older by centuries and had somehow survived several changes in technology to be the primary method of production of coffee for millions of people across central and eastern Europe, Syria, Turkiye and Iran. Maybe it was it's simplicity, it's portability or maybe it was purely culturally historical.

Leyla had arrived in a black suit and overcoat that could be considered orthodox but proudly displayed a strong Indian fashion influence rather than the traditional Russian. Once she removed her over coat the fine embroidery of the neck line, of what Eugene figured was sort of a sari, continued in an erratic pattern onto the gown to form a hypnotic flow of style. Maybe it was the way Leyla wore the garment or maybe it was the way she accessorised, minimal but for effect. It was quite striking, all this to come for coffee.

"It is a wonderful implement," Eugene said excitedly.

"To be honest Eugene we mostly just bring them out for cultural occasions. Unless you are very particular. Many of the old men will not drink coffee from anything else and believe it's part of their connection to an older more refined time."

"What put you onto this as your drink?" Eugene enquired with genuine interest.

"To be honest I most often drink tea," she smiled. "But when I enjoy a cup of coffee, if I can get it, there is something about the history that makes this my favourite. I am very grateful you take the time to prepare it so perfectly."

"You are most welcome," Eugene smiled. He wasn't past flattery.

"You coffee nuts can really talk about this for hours can't you." Will chimed in.

"Yes dear," Leyla smiled. "It is a refined art your friend here has mastered, even outside his cultural boundaries."

Will snorted. "Cultural boundaries. He is at heart an Aussie lad, not sure culture is part of that make up."

"Oh but darling," she replied ethusiastically. "I have walked the streets of Melbourne and seen culture at play, I have tasted the coffee in Lygon Street with the influence of generations of Europeans."

Eugene smiled. He loved the see someone take Will to task.

"Fair enough," Will laughed. "I like his coffee too just think that we shouldn't make too much of it or he won't get back in through the door."

The three sat under the cover of the outdoor pergola by the pool. The Azerbaijan sky had put on a show with white and grey clouds dancing openly in the azure sky. The wind, usually just short of a gale, had been turned down to a light breeze, enough to allow the outdoor seating area to provide a high level of comfort without any heating.

"So Eugene, I didn't realise you were 'The Dream Photographer'," Leyla exclaimed. "That is so exciting. I have read about your work in some magazines."

"Really" said Eugene surprised "which magazines are those? I wasn't aware I had gotten off the Internet."

"I have subscriptions to lots of western magazines" she replied. "I think it was Discover magazine that had an article that caught my interest, it wasn't so much about you but the article was devoted to the changes in dream culture. They very much painted you and your work as the future."

"He's not keen on the title, but I think it suits," Will chipped in.

Eugene sat quietly. He wasn't looking for that sort of fame.

"Oh well," he gave a resigned sigh.

"It was very flattering, not at all distasteful," Leyla said. "I am not sure why you would want to keep such a discovery a secret. I think such images would revolutionise how we look at our subconscious and the important part it plays in our well being."

"Yes. But," Will replied for Eugene. "He is not good with the limelight."

"Fair enough. The spotlight is not for everyone," Leyla added.

"I have many dreams that I would like to see more detail on. Some are intensely personal and I would not want them in the hands of someone seeking fame from my innermost secrets. So it's great that you are as you are. I am sorry if my knowing of the magazine article offended you."

"Sometimes I get a little lost in what I am doing and miss that the world has been watching," Eugene replied.

"Well I don't mind to keep your presence here low key, you can rely on my discretion."

"Thank you Leyla," Eugene nodded his appreciation. "Tell me about those dreams. The public ones of course."

"Oh I have so many. But only one recurring. I am set in an old setting, Rome or Spain or somewhere in that era, entwined imaginatively with a partner I don't know, in a situation I can't escape." Her bright smile changed to a silent reflection. "These things are sent to try us. I often think of this dream as something I should know and something I should remember, to help unlock my life, this life. But it's hard to grasp."

Eugene knew that feeling.

Chapter Four

Signposts

Leyla was a great test subject.

She was fully immersed in dream lore and had been trying to work out her own dreams way before Eugene turned up.

She listened to instructions and let the process lead her.

In the initial discussion Eugene again offered a starter seed package but Leyla asked if she could skip that without affecting the process. Eugene was confident he could and as there was no money changing hands he didn't mind a more tailored approach. It also offered Eugene a very open test for the new dream interceptor.

The resultant picture was a perfect rendition of a classic bedroom scene. The room, by the design, was from around the fifteenth century, dominated by three points of interest. A massive fireplace stood in the centre with a striking religious bas-relief depicting the residents praying in affirmation of gods grace on the smoke chamber. On the other side of the room was a large fixed chair, what might in these days be called a throne but in those times was probably used for sitting during the arduous task of dressing. The final overbearing image was of a high bed with ornate poles running to a classical hand-wrought elegant wooden canopy adorned with heavy tailored curtains. The lush velvet sheets, strangling each other like two great pythons evidence of the strenuous activity that had now concluded as the two protagonists lay exhausted.

One of the ladies was Leyla, the other was lying face down, her identity was unknown.

Leyla recognised the image from her dream but to Eugene it was new, so she gave him time to digest the scene.

"I can never clearly see her face," Leyla said. "In my dreams some nights we make love for hours, we talk, we embroider, we walk, we bathe, some nights I live a lifetime."

"Yes, I see. A common problem. Our subconscious seems to want to hide that which we covet the most." Said Eugene referring only to Leyla's initial comment.

Leyla smiled.

She noticed Eugene had a way to make his words sound like he was quoting poetry when he wanted to.

"So our next step is to adjust and uncover that detail?" Leyla asked with a ring of determination.

"More or less. Yes," Eugene replied. "That is indeed what we do."

"I have some commitments tomorrow," Leyla sighed. "How about towards the end of the week?"

"I find it best to leave some time between sessions," Eugene replied. "To allow your sleep patterns to normalise."

"OK," Leyla smiled. "Tell me the time and I will be here."

"Lets go for next week," Eugene said. "First thing."

Eugene had Paige front of his mind.

He needed to give her his full attention on her arrival and not be working with Leyla.

"Great," Leyla finished her tea and made her exit.

***

Paige had been looking through the job ads for something she could do remotely.

Marketing was undeniably something that could be done without the overwhelming need of constant human interaction. There was certainly a strong need to understand the organisation, but this could be achieved by other methods. There clearly would be an excellent option to be more external if she focused on socials. Her predominant skills were in graphics, especially social graphics but she had a good analytical background and could create and work brands with the best of them. Paige thought she may be better to look for an agency who wouldn't mind so much that she wasn't in an office in London. Maybe even an agency that was happy for her just to work part time. She found a couple of job ads and after some quick research on the companies values and ethics, narrowed it down to one to apply for now and see what happened with that before applying further.

She had decided to take a few weeks of annual leave from her current job instead of resigning. It wasn't that she needed the time to get things going, she just needed to be away from that place. With Charles gone, things were on a pretty clear downward spiral. Maybe other people couldn't see it the way she did. Social's were way down and new customer enquiries were almost nil, when just three months ago they were in double digits. Paige could leave the company immediately. She was not so short of money and owning her own apartment outright meant she had some funds to fall back on if she needed. It was small but it was all she needed. Paige's main reason for working was her need to keep herself busy. At other times in her life, when she didn't work, she found she would procrastinate a lot and get worked up over nothing. It had become quite a cycle of procrastination, stagnation, anguish and finally deterioration. Work helped to keep her focused and she found that core intention helped keep dreams from polluting her mind. These were the insights Eugene had made and she had to admit he had been right on all accounts.

She knew now that she would be better in Eugene's company. Such revelations on ones own personality can be difficult to come to terms with. Paige had always though of herself as strong and independent, within the confines of her pillars, she could challenge the world as a free spirit. Maybe that was just in her early twenties. Now, as she reached over the mid point of that decade she found herself seeing those around her as wiser and better equipped to cope all the vagaries life would spin her way. She thought more and more that she was meant to be the assistant, not the professor and she was okay with that.

As a positive affirmation action on the pending move to Baku Paige had begun to use up what food she had in her apartment. It wasn't a hard choice, she did hate going to the supermarket. Droll boring square buildings with shelves of stuff she didn't want, mostly masking the things she did want and rushing towards their expiry dates. Supermarkets, populated by trolls or worse, families brimming with bored noisy children touching and licking everything, half eating the food. Children who moved items from shelf to shelf so the running price she had in her head was never correct when she reached the checkout as the item price had only been visibly valued by its shelf tag.

Elaine had taken the time to remove a lot of junk from the sitting room and the second bedroom and either pack it neatly in a vacuum sealed bag for storage or throw it away. The bedroom was now just furniture, she had removed the soft furnishing, turned the mattress and placed two large dehumidifier packs around, one in the cupboard and one under the bed to combat damp.

She had cleaned the kitchen and bathroom and given it a similar treatment. Damp was a major problem and she wanted to protect her investment. She had arranged for her sister to drop in every month to check and take whatever steps were needed. When she first asked her sister to do that, it felt a little strange.

"When will you be back?" her sister had asked.

"Not sure," Paige had replied. "Can you just do it until I get back?"

"Sure," her sister had agreed.

"Is it a guy?" her sister had asked unceremoniously.

"There is a guy," Paige had replied reluctantly. "Let's leave it at that shall we. Please don't say anything to Dad or Mum. They can be brutal."

"Dad will have kittens, he still has his heart set on arranging something with the Chins. You know they both just have your best interests at heart."

Her sister had married within the community and produced two kids. A model daughter. Paige was not so much created in that image. From the same marble, but sculpted by Donatello not Michelangelo.

"Who is he?" her sister asked clearly not leaving it. "Are you going back to Rotterdam?"

"No, not headed back to Rotterdam. I just need you to give me some space, is that okay?" She said the last okay with passion in the hope her sister would back off.

"I was sure you would go back to that Rotterdam guy, but sure, I can do space. Can you call me every week or so. Just so I know you're safe. I won't tell Mum or Dad anything except that you are safe."

"Sure sis," Paige turned and hugged her sister.

All she had left to prepare now was her bedroom.

Paige had her clothes in three suitcases. A travel set she had purchased when she moved to Rotterdam with a roller for the cabin and two larger suitcases to be checked. She had plenty more clothes but she didn't see the point in dragging too much around. She also knew if she needed more, that procuring fashion would be available whatever far off part of the globe they ended up in.

It was a bit exciting, she had never been to Azerbaijan and had checked out some of the local landmarks. It was a bit cold at the moment but she hoped that meant she could finally try out some of her snow field clothes. They just never seemed right to wear in London and she just couldn't get to France often enough to wear them all.

Her suitcases were still open with all the clothes she had chosen inside them. Other clothes she wasn't sure of were on the bed and clothes she had decided were definitely not going to be taken were inside a vacuum bag waiting to be closed up. This was often where Paige wound herself into trouble. She could feel the conflict inside her building. She had made a decision and now she had to deal with the indecision and contradiction that developed in her head. She knew it was just her, but is it truly winning if you achieve victory over yourself in these arguments. Anyway she had made a commitment to Eugene, truth is she couldn't wait to feel his arms wrapped around her again. There was never anything wrong with their physical relationship and many of her experiences over the last year had fallen well short.

Paige moved to the window, she thought maybe she should go out, even if just for a short walk down regent's canal and around Shoreditch Park. The London skyline had other ideas and from her window she could see there would be no walk for at least a few hours. The anguish the sky had put on show reflected her own internal distress and like the sky Paige wanted to cry. She had resisted this since she got back from Amsterdam, except a few minor setbacks, continually reminding herself this would be a happy moment. Reunited with a man she loved dearly, a man she knew deep in her heart she had never stopped loving even if the entanglement of their lives just wasn't suitable at the time.

The morning dragged on and to help speed things up Paige did some more cleaning. Then she refreshed herself with some tea. She took her tea on her small balcony and as she finished the last drops the sky presented some hope, not sunshine but an abatement of the drizzle. Paige went inside and checked her weather app which showed sky clearing for a few hours. Definitely time for a walk. Normally she would go for a run but Eugene had always told her that was punishing herself and that a walk was a friendly hug she needed everyday. The canal was mostly clear, other people must have decided the break in the weather wasn't sufficient to justify venturing outside. Paige embraced the chill the rain had provided and breathed long and deep. It was a great feeling, enriching her mind and freeing her from her self generated worries.

One foot in front of the other and breathe.

Paige let the process take over and let her concerns pass before her eyes, slowly equating each problem with a solution she knew, as a partnership her and Eugene could provide. She gave herself room to grow, ski, paint and if she could create a family of her own, not a family in the sense of what she had, but a fertile environment that could be tolerant and objective, creative and free.

All of this would be possible.

The walk had come and gone and she returned to her doorstop within an hour. The rain had held and the sun had made a brief appearance just to prove it still existed and cared about the people of London. The hour's walk had turned her anxiety around and replaced it with hope and she walked through her door with that hope as shield.

Paige had some lunch and as the rain settled in outside she decided she would read for a while. She lay quietly on her queen sized bed and read from the lamp light on the bedside. As the light was low and the temperature cool that reading quickly turned to a beautiful restful sleep.

***

Around four thousand kilometres away Eugene was also feeling drowsy. The session with Leyla had gone well and he had enjoyed a coffee after, as was his habit, he had then followed it up with a swim. As he didn't sleep well the previous night, he thought a light sleep would be good before he started some further tests on his new software. Eugene was of a mind that sleep anytime must be taken. The significant eight hours is great and in an ideal world that is the goal. However, he was quite far from that and during the excitement and movements of the last few weeks, his sleep had suffered.

The private apartment he had taken within the villa had many places he could just grab a quiet moment but this time he decided it would be more comfortable to lie on the large king sized bed in main bedroom. He lay quietly and relaxed his mind taking his thoughts to a dark well where a gentle trickle of water created a rotating time pattern from the smooth wall to the pool at his feet. The well was cool but not cold, refreshing his body while his mind relaxed to the soothing sound. Before he could complete the thought, or lead his mind elsewhere, he drifted and was gone.

***

"Paige," Eugene's heart leapt.

Paige smiled so sweetly turning her lower body to walk away up the hill while keeping her upper body facing him, beckoning him to follow.

"Where are we going beautiful?" He said wistfully. It didn't matter as long as they were going together.

She blew him a kiss and continued to walk.

He was captivated and continued to follow.

***

Paige wasn't sure where she was going but she knew it was the right way and with Eugene at her side, even if he was behind her, she was sure this would work out.

She turned to face the path. It rose gently, ambling its way up the tree lined hill, The destination wasn't clear yet but the feeling she had was that it was the way home.

"Not far now," she giggled throwing her hands in the air like she was starting a dance.

***

"I have missed you so much beautiful."

Eugene was lost in Paige's presence. The smell from the trees on the hill was fragrant a mix of flowers and wintergreen, maybe a hint of sassafras, but Eugene could also smell Paige. That distinct blend of her natural body odour, her perfume and something else he had never been able to distinctly identify but something he didn't smell on other women.

"Don't go too fast."

Eugene reached out to grab her hand but she twirled away out of reach, moving nimbly across the terrain like a bird on a thermal.

The path split to a fork but he followed her closely.

***

It was an easy choice for Paige, the right fork led home. She didn't know where she was or the way, but she felt it must be true. After the fork the path straightened and she could see the cabin in the distance.

There on the verandah waving, beckoning her home was the boy.

***

Eugene woke up feeling refreshed.

He lay on the bed for a moment and reached out his hand to gently touch the side of the bed that would soon have Paige in it. The dream was over but the smell remained and he closed his eyes in the hope that putting one sense into hibernation would heighten the other. She felt so real, and she was taking him home. Eugene had not felt at home often. Even in the dwelling of his construction in the city of his choice, the dream bakery had never had a homely feeling about it. Even with Paige in it.

"Your scheduled call is due in twenty five minutes Eugene." Daaisi's new blended voice floated across the room from the speaker on the credenza.

"Yes," Eugene said, more to himself than anyone.

He took a quick shower and situated himself at his desk in the study of the private quarters. The photo of Paige had been placed strategically, allowing Paige a visibility over the bedroom, bathroom and study and Eugene took a moment to reflect on his dream before constructing the call, ready for Paige to join.

"Hello Eugene," her smile and her voice lit the room for Eugene.

"Hello beautiful, how are things?" he replied trying to match her smile, but feeling truly outgunned.

"Great," she replied. "I took a long walk this morning, very refreshing. You were right about running, walking is so much better for up here," she said holding her right index finger to her right temple.

Eugene smiled his approval.

"How is the packing going?" he asked.

"Just one day to go and I am packed, my apartment is cleaned and ready to be mothballed. My sister has agreed to look in on it regularly and she even said she would talk to my parents for me."

"Great," he replied.

"I even managed to get an afternoon nap. Accompanied by the most beautiful dream."

"Tell me about it beautiful." Eugene was always ready to listen to Paige's dreams. It wasn't just the dream, it was the narative she created around them.

"Well," she started. "I was walking along a path. It wasn't paved and it snaked through some woodland. It was perfect, cool and aromatic, heading up hill but not like a hike, more like an undulating ridge."

"Sounds very chill," Eugene added.

"It was, such a great feeling. As I walked, and I didn't know the way, I felt like I was going home."

"Really," Eugene started to take a little bit more notice.

"Then you appeared behind me," Paige said.

"You called to me, but I needed to keep us moving. I knew where to go so I twirled and danced while you followed."

"No?" She had Eugene's full attention now.

"Yeah," she said not really comprehending Eugene's interest. "The path forked in two but I just knew which was the right way and as we reached the top of the ridge I could see a cabin and standing in the cabin was the boy, you know the one I always see, he was calling me on."

"That is amazing." Eugene said incredulously.

"It is?" Paige replied. Eugene had usually been less than impressed with the boy in her dreams.

"What time was this dream?" He asked.

"Oh, I don't know. Some time after lunch maybe half an hour ago. I was reading for a little while and sort of nodded off." Paige didn't see how that mattered.

"That is truly amazing," Eugene was unsure what to make of this.

"Do you have any more detail you can give me," he asked.

"Well," Paige said with a squeak in her voice "I'm a bit out of practice taking notes, to be honest I don't write things down anymore."

"I can remember feelings more than anything and they were good feelings Eugene. Really really good feelings. Makes me think this journey is a good one."

"Yes," Eugene tried to get a grip and get back into the moment. "That's it. That's wonderful, sounds like you have it all together. Did you organise a car out to Heathrow tomorrow?"

"I was going to take the tube," she said.

"Let me organise a car, you don't want to be on the tube with all that luggage. I hope you have you winter clothes there are a few snow fields a few hours north of here."

"Exiting," she said in a trill voice. "I most certainly do have my best boarding outfits ready to go."

Paige was not much of a skier but she enjoyed snow boarding. Eugene could ski, not well by European standards but not bad compared to most Australians. The two loved to go to the mountains together.

The call was the best yet.

Eugene could see her anxiety was in complete remission and she had such a positive outlook on coming to be with him. It was not the feast or famine of emotion that she usually displayed, he would almost say she was balanced, even happy. As the call ended he reiterated that she should join this call from the airport to let him know she made it there and everything was on track.

Eugene had used all his powers of concentration not to be distracted by the fact that he and Paige had just had a shared dream. He had read about them before but had never got even close to recognising one. Reading more now he tried hard to focus without being overwhelmed. Most of the knowledge he had of them was from the Buddhists in and around South East Asia so he focused on this. Closeknit groups of Buddhists say that the same dream is sometimes experienced by multiple people, as in the case of the Buddha-to-be, before he is leaving his home. It is called the Mahāvastu and described that several of the Buddha's relatives had premonitory dreams preceding his coming. Some dreams are also seen to transcend time with the Buddha-to-be having certain dreams that are the same as those of previous Buddhas, this is stated in the Lalitavistara

Sutra a story of Buddha which tells a story from the time of his descent from Tushita until his first sermon in the Deer Park at Sarnath near Varanasi. In Buddhist literature, dreams often function as a "signpost" motif to mark certain stages in the life.

Eugene, with his scientific brain read for hours looking at studies made by a variety of scientists as well as legend, historical reference and even a bit of speculation. He wanted to absorb all he could on the subject and also set Daaisi some research tasks on the subject of shared dreaming. The detail he came up with was both colloquial and esoteric, typical Eugene.

However, concise detail Daaisi was able to extract was eye opening. She had uncovered the experiments of REMspace a Californian startup company who were using some very specialised equipment including a server process to connect lucid dreamers. The participants had been able to transfer some simple words from one dreamer to another. Eugene took some time to read the public findings and reached out to the founder to try to get more information on the possibility of this occurring naturally. It was truly fascinating to him and he pondered if he couldn't assist them in some financial or technical way.

Eugene was a solitary guy, but he didn't live in a bubble and he wasn't against collaboration where it worked for him and the people he collaborated with. He was realistic though, reaching out meant listening to other people's terms and not enforcing his will or his way. He knew this is why he struggled in business relationships and in most cases just backed away quietly from them as other people's terms were often just not fitting his outcomes.

Everyone either wanted too much or offered too little or both.

Chapter Five

Find Me

"Mate, I get it." Will really didn't even need to be told once. "I will be low key, steer clear of the locals, inconspicuous, aloof, and for a while stay out of your way with the new girl."

"She's not a new girl," Eugene smiled.

"The second coming," Will laughed.

"She's in tomorrow and I am picking her up from the airport." Eugene might have said this before but wanted it to be reinforced. "I am going to be at the airport which is risky but I just have to and the noise from Europe is not even a squeak."

"Yes mate," Will might have been listening or might not.

"What is your plan?" Eugene asked.

"Well," said Will showing he was listening. "I will be prepared with my go bag, in case you get picked up. If you do I will make for Turkmenistan across the Caspian. If you don't I will be mostly hanging out in the front guest quarters, out of the main house and with Leyla of course." Will raised his eyebrows twice.

"Great," Eugene laughed. "Not a good look," he indicated the raising of eyebrows was not required he knew what happened with Leyla.

"We will have a family dinner on day three."

Will wanted to make a rude comment but Eugene was a bit sensitive and obviously a bit nervous so he let it go.

"What's happening today then," Will said optimistically. "Time for a few beers."

"Actually I have to finish up some work before Paige gets here." Eugene had a mountain of things to work through. Daaisi had performed a lot of the leg work, but he needed to review. In Leyla's first picture Eugene tested a new software concept he and Daaisi had worked on. Truth is, it was his concept and Daaisi's work, but he was happy with that. Through this dream image search concept, Daaisi had identified a very specific painting that was on the wall of Leyla's dream. Rather than tell Leyla about it he held the information back, hoping to discuss it with her more fully during her next session.

Eugene headed back to his private area and the study he had transformed into his technical area. He knew things would change when Paige arrived and he knew she would need some space that he had previously reserved for this project. A very small price to pay. He reviewed a reply from the CEO of REMSpace, very generic. The rest could wait. He reviewed Daaisi's software changes. Mostly he just reviewed the notes. Over ten thousand lines of code had been modified and seven thousand added since he last reviewed on arrival in Baku. Most of it was part of Daaisi's self improvement and efficiency routines. In Rotterdam he had often reviewed the code but as his time there drew to a close, he found the coding of a very high quality and had moved to reviewing randomly rather than reviewing everything.

His focus fell first on the security protocol upgrades. Daaisi had improved some of the cloud obfuscation code. The visible layer had not really changed, it had just moved. Where before it was trying to make Europe and Rotterdam its home country that had now been distributed to seven different countries, all with limited extradition to Europe and no police ties with Interpol. All were in different names and had large separations between anything associated with Eugene. Eugene was happy his concept had been perfectly adapted and confirmed Daaisi should implement the changes immediately. Doing it now meant he had time to deal with any issues that might surface before Paige's arrival tomorrow.

The dream interceptor module had performed better than expected but he reviewed the notes, some code and the results in a more technical fashion from

Leyla's session. The results were remarkably better than expected. Daaisi had also identified a pathway for the safety protocols that he hadn't considered and the test on Leyla had shown they would be more effective if any issues returned.

Eugene wished he had the dream interceptor operating when he had the dream yesterday. Having that data would be fantastic.

"Have diagnostics on the latest dream interceptor hardware and software versions cross referencing my own issues last year and those of Lem Forth and Adrie Winters been completed."

"Yes Eugene," Daaisi responded using a minor nuanced adjustment to the androgynous vocal skin.

"The results are displayed," Daaisi continued. "The diagnostics show both incidents would have had more favourable outcomes. Lem Forth may have had some preexisting conditions that can not be accounted for, I have shown on screen the changes to your incidents. Eugene looked over the graphs Daaisi presented showing what happened and what would now happen, using the new modules.

"I will resume my testing." Eugene aimed the order at Daaisi but was also looking to give himself some bravado.

"Yes Eugene." Daaisi's cool voice gave him to confirmation he needed. Like Daaisi knew to reply with the positive inflection the situation required.

"Would you like to begin testing immediately," Daaisi asked. "My readings show you are quite fatigued."

Eugene agreed. He was fatigued or more importantly very tired.

"Yes," he again added a resonant tone to confirm his intentions.

Eugene fitted the dream interceptor carefully and lay back to relax. He had moved one of the couches from the entry to the study. It was super comfortable and he liked to nap when it struck him, not move around looking for places to get comfortable. His dream was simple enough. A journey along a path, no Paige this time, just him, wandering along a path that wound its way through a forest, a maze, or maybe a jungle but with walls. He really wasn't sure. The weather was pleasant enough, he might say a nice night for a walk. What he was sure of was a presence, there with him on the path. A familiar presence. His pink tiger striped snake was with him. But in a different way, less intense and less aggressive. For the first time he could hear the snake hiss gently, it was like it was hissing instructions. Eugene was making the decisions but it sounded like the snake was giving them confirmation, encouragement and a reflection of desire. Nothing was being blocked and there was no aggression to stay away.

He worked his way through the environment feeling less trepidatious, less fearful. The dream took him up, still in a jungle terrain but on an incline and now criss-crossing streams as he moved up. The dirt floor became a patchwork of jungle stone, vines and a course brown soil. At every fork and every turn Eugene felt more confident he was headed the right way. Eugene didn't know how long the path was or how long the dream was. He felt like he knew he was dreaming. A lucid dream, the snake hissing unintelligibly but with purpose in his ear. That was the surprise when the path ended. It ended but the dream didn't. Eugene stood in a small clearing. Large trees to the left and a mountain rock face to the right and in the centre impenetrable vines.

"Where did we go wrong?" Eugene spoke, he supposed to the snake but maybe to himself or were they the same thing? His enunciation was elongated, like he spoke underwater or was on a substance that made the act of speaking an effort. The snake had gone silent, actually the snake was not in the clearing. He turned and back tracked along the path, heading down the mountain again. Until he found the snake, curled up on the path looking like it was resting in the sun.

It looked up at him intently.

"Easier with her," it hissed.

The snake slowly uncoiled itself and headed down a fork that Eugene didn't remember seeing from the way he came. The fork headed around the mountain instead of up it. It felt wrong to Eugene, a task best tackled is tackled head on, not in a round a bout way. Did his father say that?

On the other side of the mountain a storm came in ferociously. Wind biting, as a gale, followed by rain, with a hint of sleet, it cut into him. Eugene noticed he was dressed in a flimsy pair of thongs and shorts and t-shirt, no hiking gear as he would usually wear. The path turned again and his decisions were clearly not good as the snake hissed its disapproval. Unsure of where to go Eugene turned and came to a crevasse formed into a crescent blocking all access from the path he turned and in the corner of the crevasse was a small shelter. The shelter was corrugated iron, rusting badly from exposure and held by wood that looked like it had been collected from the ground rather than cut from a tree. There was a man sitting in the shelter.

Eugene looked around for the snake, but it had disappeared again, maybe curled up on the path where he had gone wrong.

Surprisingly, as he was cold and lost and alone, Eugene felt very calm. The chaos of the mountain seemed to be a small side issue compared to the tranquillity that emanated from the shelter or maybe it was from the man. As he approached more of the mans visage came into view. He was an old man, Eugene would say he was in his later years, from his aspect he looked wise and·peaceful. He wore simple clothes and even though it was raining and cold, seemed to not need protection from the elements.

Was the man dry?

Eugene barely had time to take in his surroundings, as a mighty clap of thunder bought the mountain down on top of him. In the chaos amongst the falling rocks, soil and dust and the descending darkness Eugene still felt calm. He felt that calm originate from within the man who was there with him in the tumult as the whole world collapsed around them. In that calm he could hear the old man. The clarity of his words resounded in Eugene's mind as he was jolted awake.

"Find me."

Overwhelming calm and a sense of his task came from the dream and followed Eugene into that waking moment. As was his way he recalled every detail he could to Daaisi who transcribed the information and highlighted perceived keywords. The keywords were then compared and grouped and matched to known brain patterns of single and collected words. Verbs were given actions, nouns given substance, adjectives added to enhance the extent and adverbs to modify for degree. Daaisi had completed a few hundred such transactions and the logic and the execution were complete by the time Eugene sat back down at his desk.

He had taken a moment to refresh himself in the bathroom and make himself a coffee. Time well spent.

His session data showed the pink snake. The signature was very familiar but it seemed his brain had removed an element of fear and added trust. That was very peculiar.

"Focus the image on the old man," he said aloud. "I am not interested in the construct of the maze or mountain or the snake, just the old man."

"Yes, Eugene" Daaisi responded clearly.

"The brain patterns around that encounter look very lucid," Eugene commented.

"Yes Eugene" Daaisi sounded calm. Calm was not something Eugene was known for and he wondered where Daaisi had picked that up from.

"Initial render will be available in ten minutes."

Eugene decided to make himself comfortable in his private quarters. He knew he could walk out to the main area of the villa but he was particularly avoiding Will. Not so much to avoid Will but to avoid drinking, he really wanted to be clear headed tomorrow and didn't need any encouragement from his well meaning friend.

His plan for the evening after talking to Paige was an IMAX documentary on the big screen followed by some social reading in bed and an early sleep. Her flight arrived early so there would be no sleep ins. He had arranged a chauffeured car, rather than drive himself so his focus could be on her.

Paige was on a flight from Casablanca to Baku via Istanbul. Eugene had provided her a first class seat hoping it would be on time. Her initial London to Morocco flight was due to leave soon and the two had agreed to talk once she was checked in at Heathrow. That should be in about an hour. He could see the car he sent had already collected her and they were almost there.

Eugene needed this to go well and if it did, it would be due to his meticulous planning. Unfortunately the regular protagonists always let him down. Airlines were late, flights were cancelled, weather changed. Maybe that was what the dream was about. In the face of such things, unprepared but very capable Eugene was calm.

He got it. But who was the old man?

"The picture render is ready Eugene," Daaisi again, also adding an element of serenity.

Eugene opened the render.

The image he saw was a very good likeness as he could recall from the dream but it didn't help, the man was fairly generic in his appearance, a standard European bridge nose, brown eyes, brown well maintained hair and a medium build. He looked healthy even for his age which may be seventy five or eighty. Eugene looked into his brown eyes, there was something familiar about them, something that felt congenial.

"Find me," he repeated out loud.

"I have done some searching on this image and cannot find an obvious match." Daaisi replied "I will continue searching and provide enhanced search results once the fully rendered image is complete."

"Yes," Eugene replied.

"Subject two will be returning tomorrow. You should call her Paige. She is to be given enhanced access to your functions and full access to the property."

"Yes Eugene."

Eugene was excited but he couldn't detect the excitement in Daaisi's voice, so he left it.

***

"Eugene. That was the nicest ride to Heathrow I have ever had." Paige's face lit up the screen.

"I'm glad to hear that beautiful. I wanted everything to go smoothly."

"The driver was so very professional and the car felt like a glider, I suppose." Paige could have almost snorted but she held back.

"I'm so excited," she said in her trill voice.

"Me too beautiful. Can't wait to be able to hold you again. Did the check in go okay?" Eugene asked.

"Yes. All done. Only checked to Casablanca though. They asked me for a return ticket or hotel accommodation. I just asked if I needed it and they said 'no, just a service'. So I gave them nothing and I think I am in the clear." Paige was accentuating the spy craft in the situation with a slight inflection in her voice.

Eugene nodded. "The incoming flight has just landed so you should be on time. The Turkish flight isn't for another ninety minutes after you land so plenty of time. I have arranged a porter to collect your luggage and you can wait in the lounge."

"Thanks Eugene," Paige smiled openly. That melt Eugene's heart kind of smile she had perfected. "I am not so precious I can't do this myself."

"I know," he replied. "I just want you to be relaxed and refreshed when you get here. I am very sure you did not bring one small suitcase, right." Eugene smiled again.

"You said it," She laughed. "I have two big ones and one medium one. I hope you have a big car."

"I do," he smiled.

"Hey." she giggled. "Ring before the words."

Eugene could never understand how this girl could get under his skin so much. She was a little bit nerdy, not traditionally pretty but with a certain inherent beauty about her. She was educated but not in a STEM way, not something he could make comparisons with. Other girls he had met with intelligence lacked some spark, those with spark had converted it to drive and were more socially mobile than he could tolerate. It was something he just couldn't explain. Before he met her he was happy enough with his work but in the twelve months since she left, his life had been miserable. His focus on work since she had departed had born notable results, even with the obvious hurdles, but now she was back and he was truly excited. Maybe now he could finally show her more of his world, the world, and understand more of her. Change would be the key, not too much, just the parts that made her want to leave. Maybe the key was also his ability to respect the time needed for that change.

"Do you mind if we spend a few days close to home?" Paige said looking reserved.

"It would be nice to get to know each other again without having to move around too much."

"Yes, of course." Eugene was happy to hear Paige suggest that as it was his thoughts too.

"We have the place to ourselves. Will has moved to the guest quarters on the beach."

"Guest quarters," Paige coughed. "How big is this place?"

"Pretty big," Eugene said. "Only six rooms."

"OK," she said nervously.

"We can spread out or just stay in our self contained part of the overall villa. There is a gym and a pool and lots of areas you can entertain or be away from other people as you need. If you hate it we can find something more appropriate but I think you'll love it."

"Open mind," she said. "I think my time is up."

She drew a tear under her left eye with her finger and making a sad face in front of the camera.

"Yes," Eugene said. "Have a good flight beautiful. See you tomorrow."

***

Paige put away her tablet. She wasn't sad at all.

She had been talking to Eugene from a small bench just to the side of the enormous check in hall at Heathrow. It was of course just one of the four cavernous terminals that made up the greater Heathrow airport complex. Heathrow had around seventy five thousand employees which was probably more people than lived in and around the Angel. That was just the employees, if you add the passengers it would be more people than live in Islington. It left Paige feeling very small.

Before she met Eugene, Paige would rarely travel by Air. The great tide of people crammed into tiny spaces flocking erractically through the airport, crammed into security, waiting to check in, then more security and then onto the aircraft, all followed by the crash of a wave of people upon arrival. If you were unlucky ten waves crashed together and you were bounced around amongst a few thousand people all clambering to get luggage and greet loved ones. There was also the way Immigration treated you at airports, like you were a criminal, just because you flew.

Paige preferred the train. It was more punctual, less prone to mishap and a nicer ride and probably at the top of her list, train riders were a nicer bunch of people. Air travel seemed to attract entitled difficult people who felt empowered to be obnoxious to fellow travellers and airport staff alike.

Eugene had given her Business and First class tickets and that went a little way to make the journey easier, but the truth was at some stage you were always going to be subjected to the harassment of the horde. Paige took a moment, took a deep breath and made her way to the first checkpoint.

Heathrow tried hard to move the human traffic quickly and minimise the terror of the long queue, ironic really for England's largest airport as the English are the kings and queens of queuers, but the sheer number of people was mind boggling. If you could average out the people across twenty four hours it would be around two hundred people per second. Unfortunately people flock and airline schedules are mostly built around wants not needs. This would mean for peak times there could be a thousand people per second spread over four terminals. Terminal Four had four initial check in zones which eventually funnelled into two entrances.

Lucky for Paige this was not a peak time or maybe it was Eugene's planning. She took a moment to thank him and appreciate his subtle skills of organisation. She looked along the queue at the custodian of the initial entrance. A very overweight, poorly dressed, older lady who looked very much like she had been working for well over her expected eight hour shift.

"Boarding pass only. I don't need your passport," she bleated echoing the words on the monitor above her head, the sign at the start of queue and the very clear message on stand alone signs either side of her position.

"Please have your boarding pass ready to scan," she echoed not so much to anyone in particular but more to anyone that might be listening.

Chances are that was nobody. There were around twenty people in this queue and it was moving quite fast. The older couple in front of Paige handed over passports with boarding passes inside. Frustrated, but knowing it was quicker just to remove them herself the custodian scanned the boarding passes and motioned the older couple to proceed. Finally at the front, Paige studied the custodian quickly while she completed the scan of Paige's boarding pass. The black rings around her pudgy eyes glowed a deeper red as they got closer to the whites of her eyes. Those whites were a veritable patchwork of red veins and blotches. Paige considered how she would look when she reached that age. She hoped the collagen she used now, face creams, fitness regimes, detoxes and healthy eating would hold things at bay. She couldn't see the custodian having any one of those regimes and she was clearly using the cheapest conceivable makeup she could find to meet the airports minimum presentation standards.

First point clear, Paige moved further into the labyrinth that was Heathrow Terminal Four. She took her time as she had plenty of it. The signs she was looking for were to the lounge but she wasn't sure if there was another random checkpoint first so she sort of also just followed the crowd.

The crowd dispersed slightly, half breaking left and half breaking right allowing her to catch a glimpse of a digital board outlining the various gates that each traveller should be aiming for. Paige had determined that an overnight flight would require some coverage. She had put on a tight white undershirt, dispensing with her bra for comfort. She had laughed at herself, who was she kidding that she needed support. On this flight she needed to feel relaxed. She had covered the undershirt with a small tight knit beige cardigan. Over that she had chosen a burgundy over sized shirt. To match her grey fashion style pants and finally a dark long overcoat. She was nervous about how cold it might get so had a shawl in her bag, just in case.

Right now she was regretting the emphasis on cold as Heathrow was like a furnace. She was sure it was all the people so moved over to the side to try to find some space and inspected the board to see which gate she should head for. The sign to her gate said go left but the lounges were right. Now she was little confused but decided the lounges were the right place to head for. She noticed a small information booth a little further on but found it unmanned and without any electronic backup to help her out, so she pushed on.

Finally Paige found the Plaza Premium lounge, tucked away near gate ten. The upgrade between general admission and posh side of the airport was immediately visible. The young man on the desk was immaculately dressed. His auburn hair, tassel laden and bouncy, greeted her enthusiastically taking her outstretched boarding pass as a sign she was entitled to entry. His smile radiated 'welcome' which allowed Paige to naturally start relaxing.

"There is a full bar service to the right and a buffet a little further on." he said enticing her to continue.

"Thanks," Paige replied with a smile.

"Enjoy you stay Madam and have a nice flight," he called to her as she walked on.

The quiet entry hall suddenly gave way to a cacophony of noise. Children running and squealing, large men pontificating to indifferent partners, Indians talking loudly supposedly to other Indians on their telephones.

Paige moved around the main hall looking for somewhere quiet to stop. On her second trip around she decided that here was just not going to be for her. She made her way to the bar, which was packed, and to the buffet which had been stripped much to the dismay of the shell shocked attendant who had just bought out another tray only to have its contents half removed before she had a chance to put it down.

Paige decided against anything to eat or drink and moved back into the large and mostly quiet entry hall. Feeling very warm now she removed her coat and folded it neatly on her cabin roller.

"I'm sorry madam you can't wait here," the nice boy from the front desk said gently. "You need to take a seat in the main area."

"Oh," she said disappointed. "It is rather busy and noisy in there."

"You should have seen it during the peak hours," he teased. "Pandemonium and everyone a princess."

"Oh," Paige sighed.

"You might find it quieter at the gate. Let me check your flight," he said taking her boarding pass again.

"Ooo, Casablanca. I didn't notice that last time. Meeting Humphrey?" he smiled cheekily.

"Sort of," Paige giggled.

The boy looked up from his desk.

"Really?"

Paige thought she would play along, much nicer out here than in the actual lounge and she only had an hour or so to kill.

"I think it's not his real name," she smiled. "He's a bit of a man of mystery."

The boy moved his eyes left then right and his mouth popped open just a little bit.

"You didn't meet him on the Internet did you?" he enquired.

"No!" Paige replied quickly giving the emphasis to the 'oh'. "That would be dangerous. I met him at a conference."

The boy laughed. Returning to the monitor he checked her details.

"Your flight isn't for another hour," he said disappointingly. "Hey, I wouldn't normally say, but you seem a sport. Quietest place is actually in the female prayer rooms to left. Seems only the men need time with god before they fly so the room is mostly empty or if you happen to get someone come in it's likely they will at least keep the noise down and who prays with kids right."

"We have female prayer rooms," Paige asked.

"Long sad story," the boy replied. "Not a very godly story either."

"OK," Paige replied thinking maybe it was a story she didn't want to hear.

"To the left you say."

"Yes Madam past the bar to the left," he returned to his trademark smile, wiggling his hips and his hands to give her directions.

Paige passed the bar and saw the sign on the corridor for Female Prayer Room. She followed and found a beautiful peaceful room with a large semi circular bench and a large floor space, presumably for mats. As advertised, it was completely empty. Paige put her things down and made herself comfortable. She passed the time looking at some boards on pinterest. She flicked through the lingerie board and flipped through her ski bunny outfits board. While she was interested to do activities of all kinds with Eugene, she was most looking forward to just being around him. Return to the days when his understanding of her made her feel so completely treasured. It wasn't a creepy thing, he just seemed to get her various phases and have the capacity to cope with them. Eugene was one of the only people she had known who had the patience to wait for her to finish speaking and then piece together all the jumbled up things she said and answer with exactly the right response. Unless he didn't agree and then he would put forward a viable argument. He didn't degrade her or talk down to her, he also didn't interrupt.

When she mentioned it to her friends they thought she was mad.

"You're pretty Paige, you could catch any rich handsome guy, muscle bound, fitness junkie your own age. Why would you want to waste it on a guy who's most enduring feature is that he listens."

Paige had not argued, what was the point. She had let the irony wash over her and pointed at some muscle guys ass and said "Like that one."

All the girls had laughed.

Chapter Six

Breadcrumbs don't always lead down the right path

Eugene waited patiently at the gate.

He knew airports well and had taken a moment to withdraw some of his stored patience in preparation.

He sat quietly on the chairs provided, eyes glued to the exit door, waiting. His mind wandered through all the things he had to do. As a fastidious project planner, Eugene had well ordered and meticulously grouped, digitally stored, task lists but he found the list he kept in his head the most useful. That list allowed him free and open access, no need for a screen or a speaker, he could access it in a moment such as this, and ponder its contents freely. He had often reordered plans to troubleshoot a problem in the shower or brainstormed a logic issue on some code while driving. He knew it wasn't something people like to associate with. Not everyone had that skill, others had very good communications skills, some others very creative colour association skills, some great sporting skills. In his youth Eugene had possessed his fathers arrogance regarding his own talents but as he had aged he had started to see himself in a more balanced light. He could do some things and learned other things, he was definitely a good learner and sometimes he was lucky enough to remember some things too, otherwise he learned them again.

He had sat himself amongst a small group of chairs, that were empty when he arrived. Those seats didn't provide the best view of the arrivals hall exit door where passengers emerged, but it was good enough. He watched patiently solving his problems and ordering his tasks watching mothers greet their sons, fathers greet their sisters and families joyfully embracing long lost relatives. Apart from the logic that buzzed around his brain, Eugene was affected by the outpouring of emotions on display. You could say he opened up to it, if such a thing was a thing. Maybe he had missed that part of his life, something he had shut down since Paige had left and now he could finally allow to see the light of day again.

The moment her face glided out of the exit door his heart leaped. It didn't leap in time with his feet, which he got to immediately and moved quickly towards the barrier. His heart leapt in a time system all of its own derivation. It leapt vertically for a time and then randomly moved horizontally before returning diagonally. It didn't move in a perfect isosceles or equilateral, if he was to describe it, Eugene would say it was the Spiral of Theodorus, which he would then need to explain as the beauty of nature on show for no-one to see, but for him to feel.

He watched Paige turned away from him and scan the crowd opposite. He watched as her face slowly came into view, her diminutive neck turning slowly and bringing her full features from obscurity into the perfect aspect. Exactly as he had imagined she would look. He walked steadily towards the railing his eyes fixated on hers waiting for the moment she would see him. Unlike so many of the people he had just watched for half an hour he didn't call out or wave or signal. He stayed in character, even though he wanted to shout her name and scream and cry and laugh. He would leave the crying to her.

Her eyes had reached a one hundred degree scan of the room, her face perplexed. Searching, hoping. Still he walked in from the one hundred and twentieth degree slong the barrier, smiling, waiting. She stopped walking and he could see the concern brush over her face, what if he wasn't there, what if something had happened to him. Seeing that, Eugene couldn't wait any longer and walked into view with his arms open wide.

Seeing him, as predicted, Paige let a tear fall on the way to her biggest smile and, dropping her roller and her coat, ran to the barrier to take that first cathartic embrace. Finally they could let the past be part of a future reflection, not the current narrative. Eugene didn't want to let go, the time signature of his heart had increased, like a jazz band teasing a cadenza. He leaned down and kissed her, long and slow with passion that came from deep within that heart that had remained still since she left.

"*Baqajınız*" he heard from behind Paige and looked up to see a security guard placing Paige's jacket and single roller close by. The guard smiled, a happy friendly smile from one man to another. A man who knew the spiritual dominion that Eugene was currently caught up in, but needed to excuse the interruption from the mundane real world.

"Thank You," Eugene said.

In his short time in Azerbaijan he had not managed to garner even a single word of the local language even the most simple expression of gratitude.

"Where are your suitcases beautiful?" He asked looking deeply into her eyes.

She wiped her tears.

"Lost," she whimpered.

"Eh?" Eugene said with a quizzical look

"The Turkish Airlines lady stopped me at the carousel and said they didn't make the flight in Istanbul but that they are coming on another flight later today." Paige reached into her coat pocket and brandished a Turkish airlines lost luggage ticket.

"Right," shrugged Eugene. "Best laid plans."

"Must be the mice" Paige replied with a resigned air of exhaustion which made quoting Douglas Adams very appropriate.

Eugene smiled, then he laughed, then he hugged her again.

"You must be tired. The car is waiting just outside, shall we?"

Eugene was not often drawn to acts of physical chivalry. He was a pretty average guy, a little bit overweight but remained reasonably strong. Today, on the contrary to his usual adherence to protocol, he just couldn't see her walking away from him. He reached down and picked her up and placed her gently down on his side of the barrier, incorporating the action in another, albeit brief, hug to consolidate his manly action.

Holding her hand tight he then moved back to the barrier and collected her roller and coat.

"At least you have some things," he smiled leading her towards the exit. "Importantly, now you are here with me, anything you need we can get until the rest arrives tomorrow."

She smiled back at him and squeezed his hand gently. "I think I have all that I need."

The car ride home was about forty five minutes. Eugene was especially grateful he had decided to get a driver. The Audi A8 provided a smooth ride and comfort in the back that the two of them could enjoy.

"Are you struggling with the roads?" Paige enquired.

"No beautiful, just didn't want to get distracted." Eugene smiled putting his arm around Paige and drawing her close. "Plus Kamal here is a way better driver than I am."

"Thank you sir," Kamal broke in. "You are too kind."

The car journey was uneventful, which Eugene knew was bliss for Paige. She needed time between emergencies to decompress. That decompression mostly involved talking about it. So in the car journey she told him about the flight lounge, the prayer room, Royal Air Maroc, the flight to Casablanca, Casablanca Airport, the Turkish Airlines flight, for which she seemed to sleep a lot, the food and the drinks and finally some other stuff about random passengers she had been watching, some might say judging. Eugene had forgotten how much Paige could talk but it gave him a chance just to listen and absorb.

He did like to listen to Paige but perhaps unlike many other people who seemed to be listening to Paige, he did listen. She was important so he treated it as important data, he categorised it, meta-tagged it, prioritised it, if there were logic issues he would repair them, if there were factual anomalies he would attempt to clarify, at the appropriate time of course. He didn't like to interrupt and found by waiting until what he would consider to be the end to ask a question, Paige had forgotten what she had said.

Eugene held her arm carefully as Kamal delivered her roller suitcase just inside the door and bid his farewell.

***

The tour only made it as far as the bedroom.

Paige had been waiting since they met up in Amsterdam to continue where the hug had left her. She had made love to six people since she last made love to Eugene and they all had missed one vital thing she needed. Beyond being titillated, tickled, kissed, licked, sucked, fucked, tied up, strangled and smacked. Paige needed to be understood.

Eugene was the only person she knew that could manage all of those things.

She knew he was a very experienced and capable lover but what he excelled at above the other was his passion for the task and his willingness to be engulfed in her. Was that selfish of her? Perhaps, but being someones lover had two sides, getting what you needed or wanted and giving up what the person, people or otherwise you were engaged with, needed or wanted. Paige lay back, feeling very much like Eugene had lived up to his end of the bargain.

"So the whole place is yours?" she asked.

"Rented, yeah," he replied in his every Australian blase way.

"and the dream bakery?" She asked.

"Still standing," Eugene replied "But there will be no trips back to Rotterdam in the foreseeable future."

"Good," she said. "Too cold, too gloomy."

Paige had never been keen on Rotterdam, so that made her very happy. She rolled over and kissed Eugene's back, then slid down a little and kissed his lower back. He turned slightly so she kissed his hip, which lead to small goose bumps appearing all over his body. Happy that she could still excite him she turned him over and kissed him some more, teasing the prospect of a more intimate embrace to see if he could be convinced. She was impressed, Eugene was not a young man but not old either, surprisingly, sometimes his body acted like it was younger than it was. She loved the way he was, the way he moved, the way he smelt. Paige had always found fault in her other lovers but it was just that bond that made her sure having Eugene back in her life was the right choice.

The physical lovemaking lasted well into the morning.

Paige had been using her squeaky voice to entice him and keep him going, she lay in the half light now thoroughly exhausted and yet equally exhilarated.

"We will need some food," she said from within her arc of thoughts.

"Of course beautiful, the house is fully stocked. What does your little heart desire?"

"I think we need to start with coffee," she said smiling at him.

"Ah," he said. "I might know a guy that can help with that."

She watched him rise slowly, she loved to watch his body move. He was strong but gentle and his every move showed it. Maybe it was the confidence with which he moved. Paige had never quite nailed it down, exactly what it was. It was more than likely a combination of things. He put on some shorts and moved out of the room.

Paige took a moment to look around. The room was open plan with a large walk in wardrobe between the huge bedroom and the bathroom. She walked through the wardrobe and laughed as Eugene had taken up one very small section of the enormous space. The entire system was built for five or more hundred hanging items and Eugene had twenty. She would help with that.

She moved into the bathroom and checked her hair, she had the presence of mind to remove what makeup she had when she arrived before they had got distracted in the bedroom. Paige turned on the tap and added some water to her hand, fixing her eyebrows and pushing a few erratic hairs in to place.

On the way back she happened upon a full length mirror and again bemoaned her appearance. Short and bony, her flat breasts glowering at her.

Still, Eugene seemed okay with it.

She decided to test that one more time.

Walking into the kitchen she could see by the look on Eugene's face that everything she had was everything he wanted. Rarely was there something that could distract Eugene from making coffee but she revelled in the possession of such a thing.

"Shall we put a hold on the coffee?" he asked wrapping his arms around her gently.

"If you like, or maybe we can save it for later." She said in her squeakiest voice.

Then she smiled, the cute smile.

"I have some outfits to put in that huge cupboard and some to wear for those special occasions."

"Are they in your roller?" He smiled.

"Aaahhh!" Paige wailed faking some crying.

"This will have to do then," Paige said running her hands over the contour of her naked body.

"Looks like more than a man can hope for," he said smiling.

"Go on then" she prodded him squarely in the side. "Coffee is not going to make itself."

She had quite forgotten how well Eugene made coffee for her. Just how she liked it. It wasn't like Charlotte made. Her coffees were nice and very professional but as Eugene often said, his came with love. They sat together at the small table which overlooked the garden in the kitchen.

"So what's in there?" Paige asked pointing to the area Eugene had allocated for his research.

"Dream stuff," he replied.

"Right," she said. "Going okay?"

"As a matter of fact, very well. Yesterday I felt so confident I tried it on myself again, with amazing results."

"You what!" Paige nearly choked on her coffee.

"Yes, I know, a bit risky," he said. "But look at the results."

Eugene had a printed copy of the high resolution of the man on the sideboard and showed it Paige.

"Tell me," she said. "What's his deal?"

"I don't know. But instead of fighting the snake it seemed to be helping me, even if I couldn't understand what it was really doing. We were in a maze up a mountain, or a jungle and when I took wrong turns it would help me."

Eugene seemed to stop mid sentence. "Wait. It said 'Easier with her'."

Paige looked at the picture, she just let it wash over her. She knew this man but she had never seen him before.

"They look like my fathers eyes." she said, the first thing that popped into her head.

"Really" Eugene replied.

"He has such a familiar look," Paige said "Like I have known him for the longest time."

Maybe it was the coffee, maybe it was Eugene, maybe it was Baku or maybe this man gave her a very warm complete feeling.

***

Wim was getting very frustrated.

"That report is old news," he said slamming his fist on the table.

"Detective Hummel it is dated yesterday." The younger detective was nervous, many said Wim could be the next Captain.

"There is no way those men would flee to Africa," he reiterated confidently.

"But here we have a series of transactions ending in the Canary Islands, the way those transactions have made it there was quite complicated. It has taken our forensic team a few days to unravel it."

"Yes, but the fact that you could meant he wanted you to." Wim said raising his eyes up.

"Never mind. Leave it with me," he said.

"Yes Detective Hummel."

"Hummel!"

Wim turned, the only person that called out his surname in singularity was the captain.

He strode to the door confidently, but his body language changed as he crossed the threshold.

"Yes boss," he said magnanimously.

"Are you still wasting time on this bakery nonsense?" The captain was almost a beetroot.

"I have been overseeing the forensic team investigations. Trying to follow the money."

"I told you not to waste your time, just wait and they will get picked up eventually."

"Yes, but..."

"Now they have the girl with them it won't be long I would think," the captain looked up and smiled.

"The girl," Wim queried.

"Yes 'the girl'." The captain smiled a little larger, with his beetroot red face it all looked a little sinister.

"She flew to Casablanca yesterday, confirmed by our contact in the UK that she flew out of Heathrow. Our Moroccan contacts found another ticket in her name from Casablanca to the Canaries. I am just waiting on our Spanish friends to wake up from siesta and confirm she arrived and then we will put out a search warrant."

"So they are in Africa." Wim sighed. "Surprising."

"Can I follow this through?" Wim half pleaded with the captain.

"No," the captain said. "You are on the gangland cases and you are getting stuff done, so stop wasting your time on this."

Wim looked at his shoes, deflated.

"I have put that bright young detective on this. He will find them. You will get credit for your early work, but I need you to focus."

"Yes, of course." Wim said shuffling out of the room.

***

The day after her arrival, Paige's luggage arrived.

She took the time to unpack and tried to make the bedroom wardrobe looked lived in.

Eugene had organised a Ski trip for them, to the Shahdag Mountain Resort. It looked very grand. The ski season was coming to a close so she was hoping the slopes would be choppy which is better for boarding. She had laid out her ski bunny outfits and was getting excited.

There was a lot to get excited about. After there initial time with just the two of them, Eugene had now introduced Will and Will in turn had introduced Leyla. Leyla seemed lovely, so refined and stylish and so well travelled. Somehow the two of them just hit it off and so Paige had herself a new friend. Hearing of her luggage dilemma the two moved onto fashion as a subject and a shopping trip in Baku's old town was planned.

Paige laid out a few outfit choices for the day and stood in her underwear grappling with her indecision. Modern and trendy or practical and stylish. Paige pondered for a moment, she could hear Eugene moving some things around in his dream office.

She moved that way. She could see Eugene through the door and just stood watching him work. He had extracted some parts out of a box and was now working on the dream interceptor. He had explained the new setup but for the last few days had not worn it.

"Problems?" she asked.

Surprised, Eugene turned around.

"Not anymore," he said moving his eyes up and down her body.

"I meant with the dream interceptor," she smiled.

"Nothing I can't handle," he said confidently. "Weren't you going out?"

"Just dressing," she said in her trill voice. "I have time."

Paige was not sure what to think about the dream interceptor, but tried hard to keep an open mind.

Eugene had told her he had been working with Leyla to uncover her dreams. Paige didn't want to get too involved too soon so hung back a bit while the two of them completed the dream session. She knew Eugene had a process and it was better she let him work.

Eugene wandered out of the room and went to the front part of the villa. Still partially dressed she wandered into his study looking at his immaculately ordered workstation. Next to it he had laid the large Aluminium briefcase he packed the dream interceptors in, on a stool. The new design looked remarkably more comfortable, she remembered how the old version used to pull at her left ear. On his monitor Eugene had left open the image he had just rendered. It was spectacular. The inside of an ornate 15th century Polish mansion. Paige only knew it was Polish because Eugene explained he had found a painting that dated things and gave him some good geographical location.

The image centred on the bed which had two women entwined in an embrace. In Paige's all too intimate knowledge of such embraces the two looked liked they were climaxing together. It was something she really wanted to achieve but had never been able to get the timing right with anyone, even Eugene. Eugene was a great lover and made sure things weren't over too quickly he had even tried so hard to achieve this on many occasions but the timing had just never quite lined up. He certainly got closest. She looked at the two bodies enthralled, entangled and enraptured staring to a place they can only know with looks on their faces of the purest delight. Paige had hoped Charlotte might bring her that but it just wasn't to be.

Eugene came back into the room holding a small box of tools.

"Quite a scene," he said.

"Yes," Paige replied smiling. "I love the way they are both gazing into a different space, which is the same space."

"Yes," Eugene agreed. "I had never looked at it that way. Perhaps this is just beyond my perspective."

Paige smiled. 'Maybe not that far beyond mine', she thought.

"So what happens now?" she asked.

"Well," Eugene's voice changed slightly, his technical voice. Paige still loved it when he showed that big brain.

"I had a time frame and I have a place." He nodded his head slightly at the picture.

"Daaisi has started a search for historical references for both of those and potentially anyone who might fit this description in the place and time with a few referential overlaps to statistically cover all possibilities."

"Daaisi," Paige looked at Eugene with a smile. "You named the AI."

"Oh yes," he laughed.

"Say hello to Paige, Daaisi."

"Hello Paige. My name is Daaisi. Dream Assisting Artificial Intelligent System Interface."

"The AI has a voice." Paige giggled, "and ears."

"Yes" said Eugene. Not so much embarrassed as slightly put off that he hadn't introduced his AI changes to Paige a little earlier.

"Daaisi is plugged into the security apparatus of the Villa and the Dream Bakery and oversees all of the dream image collection and render, as well as a few other things."

"Wow, go Daaisi."

"Thank you Paige. Please reference me anytime you want a task performed."

"So what rooms is Daaisi in," Paige asked Eugene.

"I currently have full audio coverage of the villa and visual support where the camera's are installed."

"Oh, creepy," Paige thought about the sounds she had made in the last few days. "Where are the camera's Eugene?" This time she firmly put the question at Eugene.

"There are six outdoor security camera's focused on the front and the back and four indoor camera's which focus on the various entrances. None of them are hidden and you can access the live feed from the console near the door. If you want access just ask Daaisi, you have a user account."

"I have an account," Paige repeated.

"You do beautiful, no secrets," Eugene smiled.

"OK," Paige was going need a moment to get the AI thing into her head. "Are you an AI that would like me to say 'nice to meet you'?"

"I have several interactive audio subroutines that allow free interaction and more that I am developing everyday," Daaisi responded.

"It's nice to meet you also Paige, although I feel we have already met previously. I have just developed a lot since last time."

"Right, of course," Paige looked at Eugene with some astonishment.

"That vocal pattern is amazing," she said to Eugene.

"Thank you Paige," Daaisi responded. "I developed it myself, trying to find something unique."

"Right, confusing." Paige said using the high low tone and aiming the statement at Eugene. "That was aimed at Eugene."

"Yes," Eugene said. "Daaisi doesn't have a lot of experience with three way conversations. A few with Will but they were always very obvious when Daaisi was being addressed. It's a learning interface so maybe for a while just say my name if it's for me when its not clear."

Paige rolled her eyes and smiled.

"Daaisi has a built in silent mode, so if there is any ambiguity there should be no response," Eugene added.

"Built in silent mode," Paige laughed. "I bet you wish you could build those into us all."

Eugene laughed and grabbed Paige around the waist.

"Not a chance," he said smiling.

"So," he continued returning Paige to her spot on the floor. "Daaisi is doing a search which was supposed to be complete tomorrow. We can get the results in the car on the way to the slopes if you are still okay for some boarding?"

"I am super excited for the boarding," Paige said rubbing her hands together.

"Daaisi is in the car too," she asked.

"Yes, Daaisi is in the car," Eugene replied. "If you feel bad about that just say 'Daaisi I need some privacy' and the interface will shutdown."

"Okay," Paige looked at Eugene with a sparkle in her eye.

"Daaisi I need some privacy," she said grabbing Eugene by the shirt and pulling him closer.

Chapter Seven

Intransitive

"What a bizarre concept it all is." Eugene said with his legs dangling unceremoniously from the ski lift.

"Who would have thought to strap two planks of wood to your feet to move faster across the snow. What a kooky, eureka moment it must have been when it worked."

"It was the Chinese," Paige cried over the noise of the ski lift. "Everything cool was invented by the Chinese."

"Well, I'm not one hundred percent sure that's true." He smiled.

"Pretty sure skiing was a Scandinavian thing."

"Not," she replied smiling widely from beneath her snow goggles.

"Well, lets take it under advisement and resolve it at a later date."

"Ah," Paige exclaimed. "Not so smart when your AI isn't onboard."

She adjusted her feet slightly to face her snowboard into the light wind that had just arrived.

"We could make it interesting," she baited Eugene.

"OK," he replied. "What are we saying?"

"Skiing was invented in China. Winner gets to make the loser their slave for a day."

"A day!" Eugene exclaimed.

"It's a big house, someone has to clean it," she laughed.

Eugene loved to see her laugh, it raised within him a series of endorphins which in many other people would be considered a warm and fuzzy feeling but in him was a chemical reaction, a nice array of opioids in the brain. The last few days had been magical and with so many reasons to be happy to have her back in his life, this one could be considered quite minimal, but not at this moment.

She had adorned herself in the cutest ski bunny outfit. It wasn't something put together on the rack, it had her written all over it. Something from within her chaotic beautiful way of approaching the world. Her beanie was bright pink with the colour sloping from one side to the other towards a red colour. She had a bright fluorescent yellow ski jacket with random vertical strips of purple, blue and white on the front and back with purple at the end of the sleeves. She wore black ski pants and white boots. Under the jacket was a pink fleece to keep her warm but in a pink not matching the hat. Finally her gloves were black with a mix of orange and yellow patterns. It might not sound it but it just worked or maybe it was that glowing smile.

Eugene was, of course, dressed far more simply, cautiously and practically in black. In Eugene's opinion snow boarders always had something more to prove, not happy with the status quo of travelling at break neck speeds down a mountain they had to add jumps, twists and spins and name them cool move names like butters, grabs, and flips. Paige was not a widely accomplished snow boarder, she could achieve an Ollie but not a Nollie, a tail press but not a nose press and some grabs, but not any of the named ones. Her claim to slope fame was her dress sense. She looked good, total style even when in a compromising position in a snowdrift.

The two of them tried to take the same runs but the truth was she was better at it than he was. He also always agreed to take the board runs which were often not the best for skiers. Eugene just didn't care, he would rather be doing badly with her than better on his own. The trip up to this point had been interesting for Eugene, and not always in a good way. As was her way, Paige had decided the three hour car trip would be a great time to recount her feelings for an ex boyfriend. Eugene, as was his way, waited patiently for about two hours for the conversation to change, along the way trying hard to lead it away gently. He knew that person was in the past and wasn't threatened, he also understood she needed to get some of the feelings off her chest in a safe environment, but he really didn't need it to go on for too long. He watched the time and after two hours just stopped the conversation. The rest of the trip was taken in silence. Things had thawed when they got into the mechanics of getting onto the slopes and had lightened a lot once the activities commenced.

It had been a patchy day, some snow falling while they were on the slopes followed by glorious sunshine which cooked them in their heavy coats. After a few hours the weather turned particularly bad and Eugene suggested hot chocolate in the warmth of a cafe, so they took a break, instead of another run. Paige seemed to think that was his best idea of the day. Eugene settled the Skiing argument with a quick search and quickly declared a draw, as ski's were found in China eight thousand years ago, but much of the history leads to the Sami people in Norway being the original location of modern skiing but without skis being found that long ago. The banter between them was light and easy, mostly about the skills, runs and falls had on the mountain.

They followed up after the warming beverages with a few more runs and then exhausted returned to the car making their way to the mountain lodge. Eugene had organised a room overlooking the slopes which was picturesque but the truth was they both just wanted a shower. With only one shower in the room they decided on a joint shower which, being as it may, one thing led to another and found themselves even more exhausted than they had been previously.

Flopping onto the bed Eugene felt ragged, physically exhausted in a good way but also mentally exhausted which he remained unsure about. Quickly, sleep engulfed him.

***

The path was familiar, he knew it well. He also knew he was dreaming.

Eugene was no stranger to situations like this, the path, the forest, the mountain, the jungle. He stood for a moment remembering the last time he was here, the old man, the snake, the winding intersections. The landslide. He knew he needed to avoid that again, to get some answers but how that was going to happen he didn't know.

"Eugene."

Eugene turned to the sound of the voice.

"Paige," he replied.

"It's this way," she said.

Dreams are not so universally accessible that there is a commentator accessing stats and giving a blow by blow description. There is no script, no explanation, no predefined outcome. Eugene was used to just going with things as they seemed to need to be and at this stage, without doubt he needed to follow Paige.

He walked, as he had done before, a few steps behind her. She seemed to know the way.

Paige didn't talk and only once did she looked back. She didn't say anything, just looked at him like she had this.

They walked further, through the low pass as the gentle slope became mountains and the green turned from jungle to forest. Eugene couldn't recall the structure of the maze from last time and while he was very sure this was similar, he wasn't sure it was exactly the same.

One thing he did know is that Paige knew the way and he followed her blindly.

"Better, Eh" he heard a familiar hiss from beside him and looked down to see the pink snake to his left.

Paige stopped, turned and held her fingers to her lips then resumed her walk.

The path led up into the mountain and again the path provided walls on either side, to make it harder the weather had turned. By luck, or design the path provided protection and somehow the weather all seemed to be creating chaos behind them not in front of them.

Eugene pushed on, but somehow, Paige was able to outpace him and as she got further away she disappeared around corners. He pushed harder trying to keep up but as fast as he moved she continued to surpass his speed. She looked like she wasn't moving to fast, but hard as he tried he just couldn't keep up.

"Wait," he called. But she didn't wait.

Eugene started to feel ill, first claustrophobic and then mildly dizzy. He was unable to put his feet in a clear order, he was not strolling forward anymore but stumbling wildly. The weather seemed to be threatening from behind but he just couldn't push any harder. A foreboding came over him that he had lost Paige but he turned the corner and could see her standing in a clearing which had broken out where the path had shrunk between two huge rock formations. Eugene stopped before he cleared the small opening in the pass to look inside. It was a large circular opening engulfed in a bright ring of sunshine. The edges of the clearing dropped away in what looking like a cliff side on every side but where he was entering from showing the huge mountain range they had just traversed. The sky was a bright blue and the wind was gentle and warm.

Paige stood looking out away from the entry point to a place beyond the mountains. She was holding hands with a man. Eugene couldn't see him from the back but he seemed quite old.

Eugene tried as hard as he could to move into the clearing, first he struggled to get through the rock formations but then once he had done that his feet didn't move quick enough along the grass. It was like each blade gripped him tightly and he had to break those one hundred tiny fingers to make progress. By the time he got to Paige the man had moved forward toward the cliffs.

"He has to go now," she said as the old man melted into the clearing.

"We'll see him again soon," Paige followed the old man melting into the clearing and leaving Eugene standing alone.

He tried to say something but he couldn't. His joints felt very sore and his eyesight was regularly moving in and out of focus. Eugene tried to move again but remained inanimate, a thousand tiny blades of grass working against him, paralysing his will.

"Eugene. Wake Up."

Eugene blinked a few times and looked up. Paige was sitting above him smiling.

"It's okay, I've got you." He was lying flat on the bed and she had draped herself over him to give him more an emotional hug that anything physical.

"We found him," she said.

"Sorry," Eugene replied

"The boy, didn't you see him."

"No," Eugene replied. "I saw an old man."

"In the clearing, through the thin pass on the mountain trail," Paige said. "There was a boy, holding my hand."

Eugene stopped a moment and checked his thoughts.

"I saw an old man, before you both melted away."

"okay," Paige said not wanting to disagree. "He told me we need to find him. He said we could find him together, I am the guide but you need to provide the energy."

"What does that mean?" Eugene asked.

"I don't know," Paige looked down. "But it's a start. Can we try to find him?"

"Of course beautiful." Eugene could never say no to Paige.

***

"Detective Hummel. Can you spare me a moment."

Wim looked up from his desk from behind the five piles of paperwork that took up the prime real estate to the front of his laptop on the desk. The piles now over half a meter high, what in most paper-centric circles would be called out of control.

"Does this," he sprayed "look like I have time."

The junior detective was used to Wim's acerbic temperament and continued.

"It's about the dream bakery case," the junior detective knew Wim would want to know so was emboldened more by information than by courage.

"Five minutes," Wim replied. "Don't stay longer or the captain shall have both our balls unceremoniously removed and mounted."

The junior detective closed the door to Wim's office, took a seat and opened a manila folder.

"So," he started, "we tracked them to the Canary Islands. Both of them. She flew in from Casablanca, we really don't know how he got in but we found a hotel reservation in his name."

"Really," Wim had already lost interest.

"Yes. There has been some serious man hours go into those discoveries, excellent bilateral cooperation between us and the Spanish."

"Great," Wim said reservedly. "Good on you for forging greater European Union cooperation."

"Thank you detective," the junior detective said liberally.

"Can I guess what comes next," Wim said getting to his feet.

"Uhm, sure, I suppose," the detective said defensively.

"Well," Wim continued. "By your Tan, and your absence in the last few days, I am guessing you already went to the Canaries and you raided the rooms and found nothing there."

The junior detective looked a little shell shocked and wished he could think of way to just end the conversation now and escape.

"Yes," he said. "Did someone else brief you?"

"No," Wim said. "Anything else?"

"Well, actually, we did find something." The junior detective really did not want to continue but felt compelled the suffer what ever derision was coming now rather than have it amplified later.

"Tell me," Wim said. "Quickly!"

"We, and by we I mean the local law enforcement, found a half destroyed receipt. The receipt showed the purchase in cash of the private rental of a sailing vessel which has the destination of Cape Verde in the false names of a married couple."

"Right," said Wim. "Sounds like a lead."

Wim didn't think it was a lead but he needed the junior detective to go away so he could focus on more important things. Gangland murders had been down eight percent and he had found out local intel that might bring them down another few points.

"We don't have the resources to look for the vessel on the open ocean but we have people on the look out in Cape Verde when it arrives."

"Fine," said Wim. "They wont be on it."

"Are you sure?" The junior detective immediately regretted saying those words and cringed slightly.

"I am sure there are three of them." Wim said, "or if there are two of them they are both men." Wim stopped and went a slightly deeper shade of red. "I am sure that if this guy, Eugene Baltes were planning a getaway he would NOT print out a receipt and half burn it for your dumpster divers to find."

Wim moved towards the door and opened it.

"You will have more luck if you monitor her socials," he cracked.

"I am also sure that he is leading you further away from where he really is. I don't know how he is doing it but the lack of knowledge of the how should not distract from the truth of the where." Wim quite like that saying and vowed to write it down once the junior detective left to use it again.

The junior detective decided it would be better to take the exit as implied.

"Thank you for your time Detective Hummel."

"There is one more minute, I could make you tea if you like."

The junior detective knew the best answer was silence and took his leave quickly.

***

Leyla spent a lot of time on the appearance of dressing casually, just for these moments. She really didn't know who would be at Will's villa, she was dropping in on him in the front room just for some company. Her husband had been called out to run a special investigation on the National Police Academy so her cavernous mansion was empty. Apparently there was a major concern that officers in Baku were being hired based on family connections not merit and this was leading to a broader corruption within the force. So her husband had taken it upon himself to spend a week at the academy and investigate the matter himself. Leyla was not worried, she knew he would get up to no good. The commander of the academy was married to his sister and was an old drinking buddy of her husbands. The two would spend the week drinking, whoring, hunting and fishing and then write up some rubbish to feed to the press and those in government who raised such concerns.

Later, she had no doubt, he would revisit those people who showed concerns about this nepotism by providing them with more realistic concerns like drug possession charges, physical injuries and perhaps, to show he was no stranger to irony, charges of nepotism against them.

While Leyla no longer loved her husband, in a traditional heart felt emotional way, she did have enormous respect for his power and ability through any means to get his way. He was part of a large group that ran Baku as a personal fiefdom with a thin veneer of democracy to keep international concerns satisfied that Azerbaijan was moving in the right direction. Not unlike the way many other countries are run.

In the meantime, it left Leyla a chance to spend more time with Will, who, apart from the obviously physical attraction she had developed, was growing on her more as a constant companion.

She was even more pleased when she saw Will with Eugene and his girlfriend Paige enjoying a drink in the afternoon.

The weather in Baku was still chilly as the night settled in so Leyla had come to visit Will in a long blue dress. She had kept it loose as she knew Will liked it that way and matched it with a long navy overcoat and leather boots. The boots were impractical for a walk up the beach so she had taken an Uber. She had started using Uber once one of her drivers had told her husband where she had gone one day. The driver was new and lucky for her that day she had just done some extravagant shopping but she was disappointed when her husband told her he knew of the trip and decided to be more careful when someone else was involved.

Leyla was confident her husband would not do anything to her if he should find out she had a regular lover, she had her own nepotistic connections within Baku society which would make any attack he made on her fatal for him. She had no such confidence that Will would be spared. Will knew this and seemed to take it in his stride, perhaps that showed he also appreciated her company.

After welcoming Leyla and the completion of pleasantries, Will got up to prepare her a drink.

"I love your outfit. That blue is striking" Paige had commented

"You like it? We must go shopping again in old Baku." Leyla replied, "for long flowing dresses it is a paradise."

"Not really my thing but I would love to come anyway. I wish I was so tall and well proportioned," Paige said sheepishly.

"We each have our grace and yours and mine might be different but no less attractive" Leyla added.

"Hear hear," remarked Eugene listening intently to the conversation.

"Thank you Leyla" Paige said. "Maybe we can look for some boots, those are just so stylish."

"That's her," Will chimed in. "*Azeris* Style."

Eugene took a moment to change the subject and talk to Leyla about the search results for the latest dream session.

"So we have some anecdotal evidence that the recent render corresponds to a 15th century event. I have always been sceptical of any past life dreaming until recently and I think in this case there is also a very strong chance your dream is recounting something you have experienced in a former life."

"A former life," Leyla reconfirmed. "I have often felt there is something there. A history I just couldn't unlock."

"In this case you seem to have unlocked a 15th century illicit relationship."

"Oh do tell more."

"Wait," said Will from the kitchen of the guest apartment. "I need to hear about anything illicit."

Eugene smiled. The information was quite interesting and the matches Daaisi had made were all in the eighty or ninety percent matches.

"Your render has you sleeping with a member of Szlachta, one Emilia Borkowsky. It is likely you have recounted your tryst occurring in Lublin Castle. This painting resided there for four hundred years before being moved into the local museum." Eugene said pointing to the painting in the picture. "The Borkowsky family were close to King Wladyslaw II Jadgiello although the history of the area talks of some scandal at the time leading to Emilia being excommunicated from her family and eventually burned for heresy. Not sure how your past life fits in there, but apparently such things were quite common around this time."

Leyla sat with her mouth open.

"Not what you were expecting," Eugene said.

"Not," she said.

"I can send you some links for further reading, you might have better luck tracking down more on our lady Emilia."

"Maybe another session or two to unlock a little more," Leyla asked.

"Well," Eugene stalled a little waiting for Will to sit down and Leyla to drink a little.

"Paige and I have had a bit of a breakthrough too," he continued.

"Something that has been a bit of a struggle for us since we met has finally come out into the light of day."

"Are you coming out of the closet?" Will said jokingly.

"Not quite," Eugene said straight faced. "We have had a shared dream and some connection to a third party, which we believe is involved in our lives that we haven't me yet."

"Oh lovely," Leyla said with a smile. "When are you due Paige?"

"Oh no, that's not what I meant," Eugene said.

"Well quit the riddles and get to it," Will said trying to get Eugene to cut through the nonsense and say what he meant.

"We are going to have to move on," Eugene said.

"Move on!" Will spluttered.

"This is going to sound a bit crazy but we both had a shared dream with someone in it who has asked as to find them," Paige said. "Someone we don't know, but we know is important to us."

"I can hold onto this place or if you want something a bit smaller we can look around." Eugene said to Will.

"How long is this going to take?" Will enquired.

"Yeah, I don't have those answers," Eugene said. "You know the dream thing can be a bit hit and miss but there was a dream the other night while we were at the ski lodge that was very hit and we need to act."

"OK," said Will. "When did you think this might happen."

"We are thinking in a week or two," Paige replied for the both of them. "Eugene needs to make some contacts, although we are pretty sure such movements to where we are going wont be affected by any issues in Europe."

"I'm sure it's nothing a bit of magic grease wont take care of," Will said rubbing his fingers and thumb together in the universal sign of the power of money.

"Something like that," Eugene smiled defensively.

"I have no idea what you people are talking about but you can come and stay in my guest quarters lovely man," Leyla said to Will. "If you need somewhere. Hopefully I can be more in this moment than in my 15th century lesbian dreams."

Eugene smiled. He knew Will would be okay.

***

Eugene had bought a lot of equipment with him from Rotterdam. Having a car was very handy for being able to delay decisions on what to keep and what to leave, but the next trip would just have to be on a plane. He and Paige had decide to head East. The last dream had a mountain range that he thought was the Himalaya's. That really didn't nail it down well but a move east was a start. Eugene and Paige had talked about how to tackle this.

The snake had said she was the guide.

For Paige's part she had told Eugene about a dream she had previously about an Indian holy man. At least that's what she thought he was. That was about all she had, she couldn't recall a lot more. Seemed a good a place to start as any. India was a ten hour flight in a private plane, something Eugene could organise. He just needed to reach out to some people he knew to make sure the landing would be smooth. Eugene also needed to pack the dream interceptor and some spares and tools but didn't need more than one suitcase of clothes.

Paige said she could downsize to one also, although she chose the biggest one.

With no idea where this next step might take them, take it they would.

Chapter Eight

The winding path to unity

Paige woke up feeling very groggy. She reached up to take care of an itch on her ear and scratched the unfamiliar plastic cover instead.

She groaned a little bit.

'I hope this is worth it', she thought to herself.

She rolled over and looked at Eugene lying next to her. He was also wearing a dream interceptor, so at least it was shared pain. The last few weeks had been wonderful, he really was everything she knew he would be. Now a road adventure awaited and it was where there relationship always became the strongest. Paige knew it was her, she wasn't good when she was just hanging around doing her beauty regime, worrying about things that in all reality would just take care of themselves.

When you are on the road, even if you are staying in nice hotels or apartments, you had to be patient and tolerant. There was no place for being a princess, there was no room and no time. Eugene also changed when he was on the road. For a start he worked less, must have been something about being further from his equipment or maybe he just made more of an effort. Either way, he was great. Travelling with Eugene was always an adventure, a mix of fun discovery and action. Like Indiana Jones, without the near death experiences.

Eugene stirred and turned over.

"Good Morning beautiful," he said.

She leaned in and kissed him gently resting her hand on his chest.

"Let me get some coffee," he said quickly getting up off the bed.

Paige sat calmly working through her dreams of last night. Something in a beautiful blue stream, not swimming just walking along the side. Some strange interaction with Charles, the director of her old job, around some files that weren't complete. Something random with a Rhino and a bird on a city street. She struggled a little to remember the others.

She leaned over and grabbed her tablet to check her socials. She had made a deal with Eugene that she wouldn't respond to anything online, but he had said it was OK for her to look and that he had redirected the location services so no-one could track her. Paige had never thought of the data collected by Internet providers, social media companies and other facilitators of the social experience. Eugene had educated her when she arrived and explained what he had done, she didn't have a full understanding but got the message that looking as OK, posting was not.

After about two minutes looking at a few shorts and reels she switched to some travel news, she found herself almost uninterested in the lives of her friends. Was that bad? She had only been gone a few weeks and they were such a large part of her world, something that when she left Rotterdam last time, to herself, she used as a primary reason for returning to London.

Eugene returned with two perfect art creations in cups.

Paige looked at him lovingly. How can this brilliant man lower his gaze and take the time to make something like this? Just the practice involved alone would just be too much. It showed his determination, maybe that's what the boy meant.

Paige had run that dream over in her head so many times in the last few days. It was their boy telling her to find him, to be the guide and to use Eugene's energy. He certainly had plenty of that.

But he saw an old man.

"How do we check the images from last nights dreams?" she asked.

"I need to give Daaisi some time to render them but I was going to check after coffee, you can join me if you want to," Eugene said.

He was trying so hard to include her, how could she say no.

"That would be great" Paige said

"Anything notable?" he enquired.

"Nah, not sure," she smiled.

"I am hoping I hear from Reyansh today. He was ensuring our visa's will be in order on arrival and that we have a car and driver. If that comes through I have the plane on standby so we can move on the following day."

"Like tomorrow?" Paige confirmed.

"Could be, is that okay beautiful. We can delay if you need more time."

"Sure, oh my god I better get packing."

"I thought you had packed already," Eugene said with a smile.

"Stuff to take, sure, but now I have to pack stuff to leave here too." Paige got up and finished the coffee, she didn't realise they might be going tomorrow, Eugene said a week or two.

"Sorry," he said. "I didn't know things could get done quite so quick. In my past dealing with things in India everything took a long time."

"How was the dream interceptor last night," Eugene asked.

"Yeah, it was fine. I slept well. Could have been the pre-sleep activities." She raised her eyebrows and smiled coyly at Eugene.

"If it becomes a problem we can remove them. Daaisi has noticed that collecting nightly dreams in our regular patterns is significantly better for our mental and physiological health."

"Go Daaisi," Paige said grinning. She thought Daaisi had been banned from the bedroom.

"I am feeling good," she said. "That coffee was perfect as always. Must be shower time."

Paige got up, stretched and headed for the en-suite.

***

Eugene sat as his desk.

He knew Paige took long showers so he had gone for the shower attached to the second bedroom.

He wanted to get an early look at the images from last night.

Eugene's dreams were very clear to him and none of them related to what he wanted. None of them included Paige either so he flicked quickly through his own quick renders. The final one caught his eye a strange concoction of images, like a kaleidoscope of thoughts and feelings. It was interesting that instead of presenting a single image, Daaisi had constructed a montage, she had shaped it like a flower with small images of each thought or feeling as the petals and a large picture of his family in the middle.

"Why was the central image chosen for my latest dream render?" he said aloud.

"This is the latest implementation of the themes modification that you ask me to develop. The render is based on examples from photo memories. Does it meet expectations?" Daaisi's epicene voice spread slowly, her question forming a calm crescendo.

"Show the brain patterns."

The brain patterns Eugene saw were orderly, his brain had certainly crammed a lot of information into that dream. He checked the application for themes and thought about how to best instruct Daaisi in the differentiation of themes versus a single expressive image. How can they make the call if the car was part of the dream with the ice cream or if they were separate dissociated images. More research was needed, no doubt.

"Let me think about."

"Show Paige's images," he said.

"Yes, Paige would like to see those." Paige said walking in to the room.

"Great timing," Eugene said. "Grab a chair."

The first image flicked onto the screen.

It was a picture of an old monk dressed in purple and orange robes. His face was dominated by a large pair of horn rimmed round glasses, maybe they added to the look of wisdom about him. His tanned face had lines, lots of interesting life lines that also gave the impression he was astute and worldly. To balance his learned look he had a large round, genuine smile on his face.

"Him," Paige gasped. "That's him."

"Not exactly an Indian holy man." Eugene said raising one eyebrow. "What was your interaction with him?"

"We need to find him," Paige said.

"Okay" Eugene replied "Did he say something in your dream? Tell you where he was or anything like that?"

"No," she said, "or I cant remember. To be honest I remembered three dreams from last night, when I woke up, and this wasn't one."

Eugene checked the brain activity of the dream. It was a very constant stream, Paige was very calm and it almost looked like the monk was just looking at her smiling.

"Picture is a great start" he said, he knew positive reinforcement was better than pressure with Paige. "The robes are Tibetan. He is just sitting in a garden, nothing we can use. I was going to take us to Varanasi but it would be easy for us to relocate to Dharamsala hopefully there we can find some more information. I can also reach out to Reyansh see if he knows how we find this particular monk."

"I have never been to India," Paige said softly.

"Yeah, let's go." Eugene said smiling.

Eugene had arranged to use his UK passport to enter India. He felt using that would make it an easier pass with the two of them as UK Citizens. He also felt if anything went wrong he could keep his Australian passport as a backup.

***

The colours and the chaos of India.

Paige and Eugene had been in Dharamshala now for three days. They had taken the first two days just acclimatising and relaxing but today they were headed out to McLeodganj where the largest Tibetan temple was situated. Often called Little Lhasa, the Namgyal Monastery was among other things, the home of the Dalai Lama.

Paige was feeling very excited as they took the sky way to the top exit. She had taken some time yesterday to go out and buy some local shawls so she could make sure she was dressed in a culturally appropriate way around the temple. Maybe that helped her feel more spiritual?

Eugene's plan was pretty simple. They would just be tourists, but where they saw a chance to ask, they would show the picture of the monk and see what is said.

The first opportunity came as they entered the complex. Paige had moved to the shade while Eugene went to make a donation to the monastery. She was joined by two younger monks who were discussing something in Tibetan. When the conversation finished Paige asked the first monk.

"Do you know where I could find this monk?"

"Yes, that monk is here in the school. He is our wisest master," the young monk said.

"Really," Paige said surprised.

"Yes, really. You were expecting another answer," the young monk smiled.

"Umm," Paige said lost for words. "Where is the school?"

"Let me show you. I can show you where that master will be at this time. He maintains a very regular schedule but you might need to wait if he is contemplating something important."

"Of course," Paige said.

Paige kissed the air at Eugene who, surprised, fell in next to her. "He's here," she said under her breath. "First go."

The young monk lead them up a very serene setting along a garden path. It was very well manicured and adorned with the many coloured flags as was common with Buddhist temples. They passed the great bells and archways until they came to a quiet area which overlooked the mountains. There, sitting quietly, was the old monk they were looking for.

He raised his eyes.

"Hello welcome," he said in a quiet voice.

The bright smile on the monks face told Paige they were in the right place.

"You have travelled far my friends," the monk said.

"Yes indeed," Eugene replied. "We have come looking for a friend."

"... and a friend you have found," the monk smiled again and reached out his hand to take Paige's gently.

"Yes, Master, thank you. Maybe we search for more than a friend." Paige added.

The monk placed her hand on her knee. "Searching requires much greater energy than finding. But I can see you have that." The monk held his hands out like a bowl and aimed them at Eugene.

"Your energy bought you here and I feel you will need it all as your journey it is not at an end."

"We have shared a dream," Eugene said getting to the point. "A dream of a boy who is an old man who has asked us to find him."

"Shared a dream," the monk's face took on a contemplative look. "There is a statement. A path maybe, to show you the path you share in this life."

"Yes, a path," Paige added.

"So follow the path and the search becomes a journey." The monk's face returned to a smile, like he had just given Paige the answer.

"My dream," she said passionately. "You came into my dream."

"I am on the path, as we all are." The monk turned and looked up into the mountains.

Paige looked at Eugene. Maybe that was the answer.

The young monk returned and whispered in the old monks ear. The old monk considered his words and turned back to Eugene and Paige.

"I thank you for your visit to our temple and the generosity of your donation, it is most appreciated in our community and used to help further our teaching and those of the most venerable Dalai Lama."

Eugene looked a little embarrassed.

"What did you do?" Paige asked.

"Give what you have and feel inclined to share," Eugene shrugged.

"Wise words my friend," the monk smiled.

"I must now enter a time of solitude," the old monk said. "I invite you to stay, my novice will guide you around the complex and answer any questions."

"Solitude?" Paige asked.

"My master will now take time in contemplation," the young novice clarified.

"We were hoping you might have a clue or know the location of our friend," she said to the old monk who had closed his eyes.

"If he knew he would have said already," the novice replied on his masters behalf.

"Please come with me, we can discuss further. The master is searching for peace in this garden."

"Of course," Eugene grabbed Paige by the hand and the two followed the novice.

***

"So we got nothing," Paige said disappointed.

"Well," Eugene replied. "Look on the bright side. You dreamed a monk, we found the monk you dreamed."

"Yes, true, that is quite amazing. But the boy."

"Maybe we just need to be patient." Eugene wasn't sure but need to keep Paige positive.

"I got a really strong feeling from today's visit," she said. "He was quite amazing. I have never been a very religious person but his words seemed prophetic."

"Yes," Eugene agreed. "He said nothing specific, but what he said seemed very profound. We are on a journey."

Eugene embraced Paige tightly. "So where to, my dream guide?"

"I am the Dream Influencer, photographer boy," Paige said giggling.

The two laughed.

"I saw a photo on the wall during our tour of the monestary, it was of the old monk in Angkor Wat in Cambodia." Paige said. "I had a good feeling. Can we go there?"

"Anywhere with you," Eugene smiled.

***

Paige woke up feeling tired. The plane journey to Cambodia was not fun, if anything it was a little scary. The jet had skirted around the edge of the Himalayas and that seemed to be amongst a whole lot of turbulence. It was a jet but still seemed to get tossed around a lot more than a commercial airliner. Maybe it was just Paige's lack of experience on aircraft.

There was dream she thought, removing the dream interceptor. The snake was there. She looked over to where Eugene should have been. 'Where has he gone?' she thought.

She slipped on a dressing gown to cover her light silk pyjamas. The night had been hot, the apartment air conditioner worked well and the room had been freezing when her and Eugene went to sleep but he had got up in the night to equalise. Eugene liked the room at a mid point, not super cold or super hot. Paige was less of a fussy sleeper.

She found Eugene at his desk looking over some code.

"The snake is back," she said smiling.

"Good Morning beautiful" Eugene said rising to hug her. "Shall I make some coffee?"

"Did you bring a coffee machine?" she asked.

"Only the essentials," he replied smiling. "I got someone to deliver some milk and coffee beans this morning."

"Wow," she rubbed her eyes and headed for the bathroom.

In the bathroom Paige took some time cajoling herself awake. She splashed some water on her face and took a moment scraping her fingers through her hair to make herself presentable in a carefree way.

"That coffee smells so good," she said on return.

She sat watching Eugene prepare the coffee and then clean the machine. He really got involved in the things that he did. He placed red egg cup containing the warm brew in her hand.

"You bought our cups too," she laughed.

"Essentials," Eugene smiled. "Tell me about the snake."

"He was in my dream last night. I was having a conversation with the boy and the snake kept running circles around us hissing."

"Angrily?" Eugene asked.

"Looked angry, but I didn't feel threatened."

"Lets have a look then, sounds like it was trying to show you something."

"Render available in three minutes." Daaisi's cool tones echoed across from the portable speaker in the corner of the large wooden room.

"Daaisi is in the house," Paige said with a gangsta vibe.

"Three minutes sounds like a good time to finish some coffee and organise some breakfast," Eugene said drinking deeply from his cup. "What does your heart desire?"

"Second choice is waffles," Paige said in her squeaky cute voice.

"First choice?" Eugene queried.

"You," she squeaked pointing at him with both fingers.

Eugene laughed turning around and picking her up in a big bear hug. "We have places to explore," he said. "Old places that have lay dormant for centuries, and can definitely wait," he smiled kissing her deeply.

"Render is complete," Daaisi said.

"Passion killer!" Paige cried slipping out of Eugene's grip. "Second choice breakfast will have to do."

"Let me see what I can organise."

The apartment Eugene had chosen was an old french style villa with large ornate rooms and a lot of flourish. It had a twenty four hour kitchen attached which boasted a huge menu range from french toast to Bouillabaisse. Eugene had an order in within a few minutes and the two settled down to investigate the dream render.

"There, the snake on the perimeter," Paige said excitedly. It was still amazing looking at your dream in an image.

"Where is that?" Eugene asked.

"I don't know," Paige replied. "I remember it was hot and humid but there was a sea breeze."

"Looks like you are on the top of a hill looking down onto a plateau that goes out to sea. Definitely an island."

"Well that doesn't narrow it down." Paige exclaimed.

"I can't see what the snake is trying to point out." Eugene studied the picture closely.

"Sunset is to the right, so this aspect is facing south. Still not helpful."

Eugene and Paige took a moment to study closely and we interrupted by a knock at the door of the hotel room. A knock like that always interrupts important business.

"That would be waffles," Eugene said smiling. "This will have to wait until breakfast number two and breakfast number one are consumed."

***

Paige had never visited Angkor Wat before.

Eugene had visited Angkor Wat several times previously. First with some friends and then on his own. Paige was excited to see the old temples bought to life.

In front of the reflecting pond the two of them sat and watched the sunrise over Bayon Temple with the throng of people who came daily to see this wonder. As the morning progressed they moved to within the larger buildings of the temple.

Paige struck up a conversation with an old monk who has seen her from across the courtyard and approached her.

"Your search is almost over," the monk said.

"My search?" Paige asked.

"Your journey has still a long way to go, but you see the signs and just need to learn to read them."

Paige finally clicked "Yes, do you know how to read them."

"I am sorry I don't, I can't, only the three of you can know."

Eugene got interested, how can this monk know about the boy.

"Each has a role, yours is the compass, his is the fire, you must listen for the herald."

"How can I listen?" Paige pleaded.

"Listen with your heart, not with your ears," the monk said with a grin. "Be open to the universe and it will guide you a little bit at a time. There is so much to see without your eyes open but you wont see it without your heart open too."

The monk was joined by a few other monks who all introduced themselves with a great chatter, collected their brother and moved off into the large building behind Paige and Eugene.

Paige and Eugene were left standing shell shocked in the courtyard.

"They do love to speak in riddles," Eugene sighed.

"But, he just came out of nowhere, and seemed to know, but couldn't say." Paige turned around a bit bewildered.

"Let's just enjoy this beautiful place," Eugene resigned. "If what he said was true, it will come to us."

It took three months but finally a sign came.

Chapter Nine

San Andres

Watching the sun rise over the mountains was a ritual Eugene had taken to slowly at first.

The pre-dawn was a time of peace as the nocturnal animals found a final place to see out the day and the day shift began. The desperate chatter of the birds in the early morning gave him a great feeling of harmony. He felt the whole world was at his feet as he drifted on the thermals with the Thrush, Hornbill, Partridges, Robins, Cuckoos, Babblers and Owls. Eugene had never been much of a bird watcher before and would now count himself more a bird listener than a watcher. He was happy to sit on the rooftop and soak in the various calls. The bird song weaved itself into a pattern with the rustling of the leaves and the delicate tinkling of the wind chimes that were strategically hung around the house.

It had been a full month that he and Paige had been residents at the foothills of the Phnum Aoral Mountains. Before that a month in a lodge around the shores of Tonle Sap and before that a month in and around the Siam Reap and the Angkor Wat complex.

Answers were not coming, but there was no imperative. Eugene was very happy just to spend the time with Paige.

Their renewed relationship had developed and matured. There was never any shortage of love for each other, but relationships are more than that and it was those things that needed to consolidate for there to be a long term future. There was no doubt that just having each other was a big bonus. Paige, in her own words, was often torn apart by the cruel words of other people. She was especially wrecked when people were overly critical, sarcastic or bombastic about her choice of partner. She still had contact with those people, her sister, her family, her friends but most of them were blown away that she was in Cambodia or Azerbaijan or India. Some of them asked her pretty detailed questions and gave very open opinions back but mostly those words were not snide or bitchy. She spoke to Eugene about it a lot and that in itself was probably the core to the strength they were building. When she received feedback that made her nervous this was not the right path for her she turned to him to see what he said.

From Eugene's point of view he could spend the rest of his life this way. He ate more healthy, exercised better, he could research freely and travel. He was enjoying being less driven and more in tune with the moment. He and Paige had spent the time in the region exploring. They had seen a lot of Cambodia, Laos and Vietnam but had also ventured to Thailand, Malaysia and Indonesia on short trips. Eugene was feeling pretty confident that they would not be setting off any alarm bells in Europe moving around these countries. Any Interpol order out for him would only take affect if he hit Europe so avoiding that was going to be key. So far it had been a storm in a teacup.

If it became a problem he would address it, but for now he just relaxed. At night wherever they were, he and Paige would turn to their dreams in hope of a clue to what the next step was. Sometimes their dreams were shared, sometimes they were alone but one thing became clear as the two became closer, the happier moments were reflected in the dreams they had. Maybe in this happiness the boy didn't want to appear or intervene or maybe they needed to be happier. Paige said she had seen the boy but his messages were not clear. Eugene had tracked the images around those five interactions. Each time the boy is standing in a clearing if the sun in the west looking out over the ocean or if its in the east looking at a hilltop. The old man seemed to not want to appear, at least nothing that Eugene could remember and nothing that Daaisi picked up in their brain patterns using the new code developed just to highlight this in particular.

Eugene returned inside the house. The sun had risen and the birds had gone about their business leaving him to prepare for the morning. Eugene liked to run through a round of isometric exercises first and then set himself a five kilometre bike ride and a five kilometre walk everyday. He had picked up some gym equipment cheap and had moved it with them as they moved around

Cambodia. It was more convenient to exercise in the house than move around the local community. They were in a remote area but most parts of Cambodia has someone in it and you are never sure of their intentions, so safety first.

After completing his morning exercise Eugene made his way to the kitchen to fire up the coffee machine. Not being a morning person Paige was still sleeping, she had tried to get up with him to see the sunrise a few times but had returned to her long sleeping patterns after feeling the effects of early rising on her exercise routine. Paige was an afternoon jogger, as Eugene couldn't, the treadmill was a very big bonus once they moved away from Siem Reap.

Moving down stairs to the kitchen Eugene started his process to make coffee's for both he and Paige.

While he was waiting for the coffee machine to heat up, he took a quick look of the night times dream images. Nothing, again. He thought about the last time Paige had seen the boy and checked the image again as he had done almost every day. How frustrating to be so close and yet see nothing.

The boy stood side by side with Paige as they were looking at something. It looked like the ocean to Eugene but it could be a sea or possibly even a large lake. It was a body of water, not much of a clue.

He looked again, scanning the unusual light patterns around the feet of Paige and the boy.

What was that?

The coffee machine was ready to be used and gave a little hiss to display its irritation at his delay. Eugene did miss his coffee machine in Rotterdam. He completed the grind, the pack, the pull and the milk steam with his usual flair of art and precision producing two coffees beautifully adorned by a pair of swans. Moving upstairs again to the bedroom he opened the door to find Paige buried in a mountain of bed covers and sheets. Eugene like to keep the temperature moderate and sleep without clothes or a sheet, Paige liked to be well covered, perfect bedfellows and here she was.

"Coffee, beautiful," Eugene said gently.

"Yes, coffee!" She cried out, almost enthusiastically from underneath her fabric retreat.

"I was thinking," Eugene started.

"I was also thinking," Paige replied quickly. "That you should hold that thought until after I have had at least one coffee."

Paige popped her head out of the sheets with a smile. Eugene handed her the cup and she gazed on the artistic swan lovingly.

"Aww, that's so gorgeous," she cried.

"How were the birds?" Paige asked.

"They always put me in the best frame of mind." Eugene admitted.

"Give me clarity" he smiled.

That was the truth, simplicity can often bring clarity to complexity, just ask Mozart.

"So what clarity did they offer to our current problem, tweet tweet." Paige gave her best bird impression whilst gently ingesting her first few mouthfuls of coffee.

"Well none," Eugene said. "But I looked at the last image of the boy and I think the shadowing is all wrong."

"Whoa," Paige cried out. "Remember," she said pointing to the coffee with a smile.

"Oh yeah," Eugene said feigning a frown. That smile could still stop him in his tracks.

"That sounds like a great 'after shower' conversation." Paige added moving from underneath the last sheet and walking naked to the bathroom.

"Hey," he said. "Not a fair distraction play."

Eugene sat on the bed and waited for a moment. He wanted to go into the bathroom, take off all his clothes and join her, but her knew better. It wasn't that he couldn't, she was in a good mood and Paige wasn't just accommodating she would also enjoy the experience. However, Eugene had more important things to discuss and he knew that a moments distraction would mean they would lose focus, lose track. Maybe that's why they were three months in Cambodia with little to show but a strange conversation with a monk. They got that in India in less than a week.

Paige's idea of a quick shower was fifteen minutes so he had time to think through what to say, how to present it properly. He knew it wouldn't be palatable to her. The last time they had been down this path it had nearly cost him his life and her, her sanity.

'But the process had improved so much and the technology was now safer than ever'.

'The dream interceptor had a fail safe now'.

'It's linked to a whole bunch of physical and mental parameters'.

'I would monitor the process to make sure you are safe'.

'You know I wouldn't let anything happen to you beautiful'.

'You know I wouldn't let anything hurt you beautiful'.

'You know I would never put you in danger beautiful'.

The thoughts sounded like a hard echo even in his head.

'There is no way she would be convinced with that tactic', Eugene thought.

He chastised himself. Putting her in harms way is exactly what he was proposing.

"Am I interrupting," Paige said appearing from the bathroom wrapped in a towel.

Eugene smiled. Even if she was, it was fine.

"So tell me," Paige said.

"Well, I found some shadowing that is inconsistent in the last image of you and boy," he said.

"Inconsistent?" she asked.

"The sun is setting in the west, so the shadow should be behind you, but it was at your feet meaning it was noon and his shadow was in front of you meaning the sun should have been in the east."

"Is the dream render that accurate," she asked. "Does it usually get those things right."

"Surprisingly, it does," Eugene said feeling a little bit proud.

"So you are saying my dream wasn't technically accurate, but it wasn't the technology, it was something I did?" Paige looked a little perplexed by where the conversation was going.

"No, not quite," Eugene replied.

"Maybe not something you did, maybe a clue for us to look further."

"Sorry, not following," Paige had no idea what Eugene was talking about.

He quickly recounted the incident where one of his former study subject's Lem had dreamed a reflection in a mirror that showed a newspaper headline which he at first had overlooked as unimportant but then later had used it to find out an important date.

"Right, gotcha," Paige said. "You think there is more there we are not seeing and ..." she stopped and raise her hands to form a question.

"I think we should use some stimulation to better investigate the dream," Eugene said.

"Oh," Paige said now understanding what the conversation had been about "but I thought that was not, you know, healthy."

"I have made lots of modifications, put in some fail safes, improved the dream interceptor and software. I think its much safer now." Eugene wasn't even convincing himself with those words.

"We have been using the dream interceptors for months now with no ill effects."

"How many people have you used this procedure and the new tech on?" Paige asked.

"Yeah, about that," Eugene said. "No-one, well sort of Leyla."

"So I am back to being guinea pig number two," Paige frowned.

"In this case you have moved up the list," Eugene tried to smile.

"But you just said Leyla?" Paige looked a little unsure. "Am I one or two?"

"New version, so that's makes you number one," Eugene said his face starting with a semi smile but falling away to nothing.

"Let me think about it," she said. "I might need some breakfast."

"Of course, beautiful."

The day went on as had any other in the last few months.

Breakfast was a long grazing affair, a series of seeds and nuts, freshly squeezed fruit juice and fresh fruits. By the conclusion of the meal barely a word had been said that wasn't restricted to the process of preparing and eating. Paige was not looking to engage and Eugene really didn't want to push the idea.

If it was his dream he would be asking her to care for him while he stimulated his own mind, but it wasn't.

***

After breakfast, Paige retired to the lounge area to look through some social media. Even though she wasn't working, Paige liked to keep up with some of the industry trends that were happening, mostly from YouTube, Instagram and pinterest. She had intended to work but the momentum had swung wildy when she was with Eugene. This all seemed so much more important. She had taken a keen interest in where they would go next and figured if things didn't break here she was thinking the next destination should be another ski field. She did a little travel planning, knowing that there would be no skiing in Europe she looked at Korea and Japan and was impressed with the fields she saw, especially in Japan.

Paige was really just looking for any excuse to get out of what she was pretty sure she was going to need to do.

At one stage she tried to recall how bad it was last time.

It wasn't so much the process it was the after effects. The actual dreams were just more intense and more focused but in the days and nights following there was generally a brutal follow up of headaches, lethargy, aching muscles and confusion.

Paige recalled one dream when Eugene had tried to get her to focus on a simple table in the corner when her dream was initially focused on the kitchen as part of one of her daily life dreams. The process of moving her gaze piece by piece was a bizarre and took just three sessions over three days but in the week that followed she had ragged erratic dreams of running off cliffs and falling in long dark chasms. The dreams were of epic proportions driven by elongated terror which after a few days returned to normal, whatever that was for Paige. Did she want to sign up for more of that.

No Thanks.

But that wasn't what Eugene was offering, she knew that, she knew he was smart and once he saw a problem he fixed it. She had pretty much already decided to go ahead but thought maybe taking a little time and not being so eager to just say yes might be good way to balance the power in the relationship. Paige really appreciated Eugene's strength and his intellect but that didn't mean she had to be jelly. Jolted back to consciousness after a nap moment Paige sat in the hammock thinking carefully about how to move forward.

"Daaisi," she said hopefully.

"Yes Paige," Daaisi responded courteously. Daaisi had not been restricted from the lounge, just the bedroom and bathrooms. "How can I assist?"

"Can you tell me about the improvements made in the dream interceptor and seeding process since the last time I was used as a test subject?"

"Of course Paige" Daaisi responded "What format would you like the response. For me to list out all the changes will take longer than three hours. I could do a top ten in a list or those of maximum importance to establishing subject health."

"Yes" said Paige "I am interested in changes to do with subject health."

"No problems. First, the dream interceptor had its primary capacitor moved from a position over the posterior cingulate cortex to a more central cranial alignment to minimise the affect of a certain level of electric charge may have during particularly complex dreams, especially those involving animal totems."

"Right," said Paige "So I am still dreaming of my animal totem. Can you quantify the effects now compared to the effects then." Paige said hoping that it made sense.

"Yes. There is a three hundred and forty seven percent drop in manic brain activity since the capacitor was relocated."

Paige stopped. "Three hundred and forty seven percent," she said.

"Yes Paige," Daaisi's voice sounded so impassive.

"Second, there is now a primary directive that should manic, complex or dangerous brain patterns arise beyond a safe threshold inline with known biometric levels an orderly shutdown procedure is undertaken to minimise the mental and physical health to the subject."

"Great" said Paige "Has this been successful on other subjects?"

"Yes Paige. There have been mixed results. There was significant success on all but one subject"

"Right" said Paige. She knew about Adrie's stroke.

"Do you feel there is a chance of that happening again?" Paige asked.

"I can't answer that question as it contains too many variables that have high probabilities of being incorrect." Daaisi's reply said it all.

"Is there a number three?" Paige asked.

"Yes," Daaisi continued. "The new version of the dream interceptor added a number of health parameters that were not available previously. I can now study over one hundred biometric data points and, especially for subjects such as yourself for which I have an extensive data set, make comparisons that will allow the orderly shutdown procedure to commence before any damage takes place."

"Oh jolly good. One more question," Paige smiled.

"Does Eugene already have a plan worked out how we are going to do this?"

"Yes Paige," If such a thing was possible Paige detected a smirk in Daaisi's tone.

"… and what are it's chances of success," Paige added.

"That is a second question, currently the chances are close to ninety five percent success."

Paige was a little taken back. Did the AI just dis her counting?

She decided she would be better off talking to Eugene and moved quietly to his study.

"Did you get the answers you wanted?" he asked.

"Yes," Paige replied. "We can start tomorrow."

***

Paige was a little drowsy. The process hadn't fixed that. Eugene was siting beside her, holding her hand. She stayed where she was and let her eyesight adjust.

"How did I go?" she asked.

"Perfect," he replied.

"Do you have the results already," she asked.

"No," he said. "Not yet but the results aren't as important as the fact that you made it through with 'flying colours' as you might say." Eugene had a big smile on his face.

"Ninety five percent chance," she replied. "I did note the coffee is a little slow arriving."

"Right," Eugene said getting up and moving to complete his most crucial task.

Paige tried to recall what she saw but all she could recall was that it was him. After a moment she got up and moved to the kitchen where he was just finishing up the coffee. She knew the overall process was about ten minutes, to get the image and the coffee, only Eugene would time such things to perfection. The coffee was presented to her and as he planned it would be the image came up on the TV in the kitchen.

"It's you," Paige said quizzically

"Yes," Eugene replied. "Seems it was my shadow."

"But you weren't dreaming that." Paige said "I really am going to need this coffee."

115

"Yes," Eugene agreed. "I think this may take some unravelling."

***

It had been a frustrating week.

Eugene wasn't able to access that dream. It was clear he was there, at least Paige had projected him there, but he had no way to get there, no way to start. He couldn't stimulate with no starting point and, even though he had tried nothing seemed to have worked. Another dead end. Eugene lay on the bed feeling both at peace and also frustrated. This place was magical and he really didn't want to move on but if they couldn't gain any traction maybe that was the next step. Paige was lying next to him looking at her tablet. He knew she shared his frustration.

They had taken a long walk up one of the mountain tracks to a small temple carved out of the rock face. It looked like it had started as just a small prayer table and over some generations been built into something larger. The two of them had sat for a few minutes to share the tranquillity and the majesty of the site before heading back down. The whole operation a few hours of hiking was tiring but rewarding. She turned and kissed his cheek, her hands gripping his hip and turning him over to face her.

"We just need to follow our hearts," she said smiling "Where does your heart say?"

Eugene learned forward and kissed her long and slow.

"My heart just wants to be with you," he said.

They made love in an impassioned moment which drained what remaining energy they both had and fell into a deep sleep.

***

At first Eugene wasn't sure where he was. Then Paige tapped him on his shoulder.

"Finally we are here together."

"All of us," came a voice from behind.

Eugene turned to see the old man.

"Where are you?" Eugene asked.

The old man turned and sat on a bench near a shack made of rusted tin.

Eugene looked past the shed and just saw the ocean, he turned the other way and just saw some hills. He turned to Paige, "how can we find him?" he said.

"We need to remember that ship wreck," she said pointing behind Eugene.

***

"We need a list of all metal hulled cargo ship wrecks off islands in the tropics that you can find pictures of," Eugene issued an order like all future problems were going to be solved by this one thing.

He was determined that, if Paige saw the island from her dream while conscious she would remember so once she had showered, he had roped her into looking, while he made her breakfast. Paige had agreed to go along with it but had said they should also replicate yesterday's activities but this time remember to put on the dream interceptors before they fell asleep.

The stream of images of great hulking shipwrecks slowly cascaded across the TV screen for Paige's perusal. Many of them were commercial vessels that were abandoned after being beached in bad weather, some were military, maybe from World War II.

"How many of these are there?" Paige asked

"There are three millions vessels but only twelve thousand meet the other criteria provided," Daaisi replied.

Eugene smiled. "I will make more coffee."

It was a long shot but worth a try.

The old mans face had been so rough, so real. Eugene thought he could smell his breath and his voice had a strong timbre about it. His accent sounded Creole but maybe some Spanish, Eugene's experience in that region of the world was pretty limited.

He prepared some fruit, squeezed some orange juice and put together a range of nuts and grains for Paige. He had found some grapefruit at the local market which he was enjoying so included it hoping she would enjoy it too. He knew she didn't want to look at the images but she was as invested in this as he was. It was over an hour before she had to get up to use the bathroom.

"How many images is that?" Eugene asked Daaisi while she was gone.

"We have completed twelve hundred of the images available," Daaisi said impassively.

Paige returned and gave a smile.

"Some green tea?" Eugene asked.

"Sure," she said smiling.

The images began again as Eugene put together a tea pot of green tea and placed them on the small table in front of the couch Paige was sitting on.

He was in mid motion placing them when she got up, sending the whole tray tumbling to the floor.

"That one," she cried "The big square looking one."

Daaisi had cycled back an image and the hulking form of a large rectangular iron freighter sat on the screen.

"Where is that?" Eugene asked.

"Cayo Rocoso, San Andreas, Columbia." Daaisi replied.

Chapter Ten

Cedar Point

Eugene was nervous about the trip ahead.

He had previously travelled to the Caribbean a few times and one trip to Brazil and another to Argentina but he had never ventured into South America's central countries. They had always seemed a bit out of bounds, maybe a bit dangerous, maybe a bit difficult. Paige added that she had never even considered there might be anything worthwhile there.

All the commercial flights between Thailand and Columbia seemed to go via Europe. He didn't really want to risk even a touchdown, where something, however minor might be all it took for him to be taken into custody. He was still a little worried about the authorities in Europe, particularly from the police in Rotterdam. He suspected they had let it slide and Daaisi corroborated that as there was no change to his status of 'at large, but wanted for questioning'.

To be sure, and give himself piece of mind, he and Paige made their way back to Thailand first and he made some very deliberate financial transactions, which if anyone was watching would show up clearly alerting them to his presence in Bangkok. Eugene had shutdown all but one of his old trading mechanisms deliberately. He wasn't sentimental, he had closed all the old accounts and moved the money somewhere else. This one was the only one left with any link to Rotterdam or the dream bakery and he had kept it just to do things like this. He figured it was being monitored, police were not subtle.

Using this account he purchased some flight tickets to Athens in the hope that would give the police some breadcrumbs to follow. Whether it worked or not it was money he felt better spending. In contrast he used some cash to arrange another private plane. There was no way a private plane would make it the whole way as a single flight leg, so a stopover was needed. Eugene figured his best chance of avoiding problems was the leave the private jet on the runway, that would avoid any need to break immigration. The obvious choice was Dubai or Abu Dhabi where this would be normal.

He reached out to his network and found an agent in Columbia who could take care of the ground handling on arrival. Easiest way was to get immigration to come to the plane in Bogota and then they were free to fly on as a domestic flight to San Andreas.

***

Paige had to pinch herself, again. She had seen photo's of private jets like this, rock star style. She certainly never thought she would be travelling in one. She leaned back in one of the big lounge chairs at the front. The first leg had been fun. A mid morning take off, some lunch, an afternoon champagne. Some socials browsing and a catch up on the Anime she was watching before they arrived in Abu Dhabi, on time. On time was important for Eugene, she didn't think it mattered too much. Paige had enough travel experience to be able to do medium flights without any ill effects at all, but she wasn't sure how she would go on the next leg, eighteen hours was a long time.

She had to admit it was an amazing experience not only for the travel itself but also for the interaction at the airport. There was no queue's and no check in, well none she participated in and immigration was quick. The most airline like was when her handbag was security scanned but there was an usher to do that. The aircraft, a Gulfstream G700, was decked out for long haul travel. It had large first class style lounge chairs that would lay out flat like a bed in the front for take off and landing, a lounge area with large TV, bar and kitchen in the mid section, a large double bedroom and very spacious bathroom with shower in the back.

She had chastised Eugene when they got on board.

"Too much," he had asked.

"Way, way too much," she replied.

"All the commercial routes seem to go via Europe," he complained. "So it seemed appropriate. At least we will be comfortable."

The jet also came with a flight attendant. So, after the most comfortable of flights between Bangkok and Abu Dhabi and a refuel, they set out for Bogota.

This eighteen hour leg allowed them some sleep and they took the opportunity to change their eating to match the Colombian time zone. So very different than having airline food crammed into you whenever they felt like serving it.

Paige was thinking there would even be time to join the mile high club in style.

***

Eugene couldn't have asked for things to go better. He figured, you spend the money, you get the service. He had an affliction to mass travel and now he had found this, it was the way to go. He couldn't believe how relaxed Paige was. Normally mass travel with her was not the easiest of experiences. She would feel unwell or bored or claustrophobic or get hay fever or any other number of phantom illnesses that only came up in airports. He knew she was happy when they retired to the bedroom. She had gone to shower a little early and was waiting for him in a thin purple silk negligee he had bought her for her birthday.

They woke up to breakfast in bed.

As planned there were no issues in Bogota. Two immigration officials came on the plane to inspect passports and luggage and gave them clearance to move on. The agent had already submitted all the necessary fees and paperwork. The short, two hour flight between Bogota and San Andreas gave Eugene a much needed picture for where they were. The flight trajectory was much lower, allowing for a clear view of the major national park in the north of Columbia. The flight banked around the coast of Panama before moving into the open Caribbean sea.

Eugene was fascinated that the Island of San Andreas, an English Puritan colony at one stage, was much closer to Nicaragua or Costa Rica or Panama but had ended up with Columbia as the result various disputes. They landed in San

Andres at around six in the afternoon. Eugene had organised a car to take them to the accommodation at Casa Iguana del Mar, a beautiful Villa on a large private compound on the quiet side of the island. So far things had gone well, like they were meant to be there.

***

Paige slowly opened her eyes.

It was dark, but in the dim glow of the LED from the air conditioner she could see the outline of the room. She tried to recall where she was and came to the conclusion it didn't matter. The familiar form of Eugene lay next to her, breathing lightly as he did, a calming effect even as he slept. She looked up at the air conditioner, it was new and had the temperature illuminated, that was why the light was so bright. She felt a little hot but the temperature said 23C. The events of the previous day, or was it more than a day, came back to weave its way into what conscious thoughts she had retained.

Yes, San Andreas, Columbia.

She hadn't built up the courage to tell any of her friends or her parents where she was going before hand and was still thinking about how she was going to tell them, now she was here.

One message to her sister. "Taking a Gulfstream to Columbia. Don't worry about me."

She hoped it would be enough.

Paige fumbled beside the bed in her handbag and extracted her tablet. She turned it on and lowered the screen brightness to hopefully leave Eugene sleeping. It was unlikely, but worth a try. He was such a light sleeper. She had seventy three messages on Instagram. Oh Shit, twenty one from her sister. Most of them were just expletives. She had seen a few come in on the flight but just didn't have the answers at that time, so she left it. She knew that wouldn't cut it for very long. Oh no. A message from her Mum, much harder to ignore or push under the electronic carpet.

Eugene stirred, turning and draping his arm over her belly.

"What time is it?" he said.

"Three am, here," she replied.

"Lunch time in Cambodia, yesterday when we left."

Eugene laughed.

"Tricky to keep track," he said.

He almost seemed to be fully awake, she wondered at the way he could do that, from sleeping to alert in one step. Paige needed to open one eye at a time, take a few moments in between and preferably have some tea or coffee before being asked to function.

She knew he would offer coffee soon.

"What an amazing trip that was." he said. "I have never done anything like that before. Shell sent me on a few private flights but nothing that outrageous."

He moved slightly onto his side and moved his hand up to her chest cupping her small breast with his hand.

"So happy we got to experience it together," he said.

"This journey..." he stopped when her finger came down on his lips.

Paige dropped the tablet on the bed and turned to kiss him. It was 3am and she knew her breath was bad, she probably even smelt bad because they didn't get a chance to shower when they arrived, they just found the bed and slept, exhausted.

Now she wasn't exhausted and wanted so much to make love to him, to hold him.

***

Eugene could work out most things. He was especially good with tech. He was also pretty good with coffee. All of these things were true. So why could he not work out this machine. He had managed to get the coffee out but the milk wand was electronic and seemed to want to make hot water not steam.

He had left Paige in bed asleep.

"There is a delivery van arriving at the front courtyard." Daaisi's voice emanated from his mobile phone.

"Do you have perimeter security?" he asked.

"Yes Eugene, I have full visibility of the front of the structure," Daaisi replied.

Eugene quickly moved to the front of the house and after checking the security camera outside opened the door.

"I have a delivery," the young man said. "Royal Enfield Meteor for Eugene, is that you?"

"That's me," said Eugene with a smile.

"Nice bike, my man," the delivery guy looked excited.

"It doesn't seem to be a big island," Eugene replied.

"Hey man, wow," the delivery guy looked excited. "Is that an Australian accent?" he exclaimed. "That's so cool. Oh Sorry man, we don't get a lot of Australian's here on San Andreas."

"No problems" Eugene replied, sitting on the Meteor to try it out. "Are you from here?" He sat in the riding position on the bike making sure his natural grip and stance would suit the bike's shape. As he suspected it had the perfect fit for him.

"Born and bred," the man was in his early twenties with a deep tan and long wavy brown hair.

"I wanted to get to Cayo Rocoso but didn't really want to flock with the other tourists. Is there a way to get a private boat out there?"

"Absolutely man. My cousin Juan has a luxury sport fishing yacht I can get him to call you if you like. It's a sweet ride, a big sleeper for big game fishing." He quickly pulled out his cell phone and showed Eugene a picture. "But this is not the season." he continued, "so I know he will do you a good deal on going out to the rocks and hanging around."

"That would be great," Eugene replied.

"Your first time on the island," the young man asked.

"It is," said Eugene. "Looking for this old guy." Eugene held up a picture of the old man from his dream.

"Oh right," the delivery guy took a good look. "Nope, don't recognise him. I'm from North End so maybe he is La Loma or San Luis, lots of small settlements there, those folks don't get involved outside their own small community."

With eighty thousand people on the island, it was a long shot.

"My name is Roberto, here is my cell number, I have to head out, a few more deliveries to make this morning, very sure none will be as sweet as this," he said patting the seat of the Meteor.

Roberto drove off up the path and Eugene turned to go back to the coffee.

Paige was lying in bed with the sheet over her head.

Eugene pulled it back slightly to see her staring up at him with tears in her eyes.

"Whats wrong beautiful."

"I am so happy," she cried.

"Nice way to show it," he smiled at her.

"But," Paige sobbed. "How do I tell my Mum?"

"Oh yeah, right" Eugene knew something like this was coming. To be honest he expected this in Cambodia, but it was just so perfect. Clearly, Paige had been putting it off.

"I honestly think the truth is the best option," he counselled her carefully.

"The truth," she burst into sobs. "This truth is fantastic, but its not a truth she could swallow. That plane ride, the villa in Cambodia, the places we have been."

"So when was the last time you told her what you were doing?" Eugene asked.

"I didn't even tell her when I left London." Paige let out a big heaving bawl.

Eugene was surprised. "I thought you were talking to her in Cambodia."

"No," Paige almost seemed to howl.

"Okay, Let's get this into you," Eugene said. "Then we can work out a plan and you can call her. It's five hours time difference so it's lunch time in London."

Paige sobbed a little and took a sip of the coffee Eugene had presented.

"You should just apologise to her and tell her the truth. The truth about us, the truth about here."

"The truth. Following a dream sounds romantic, but literally following a dream, or a few dreams sounds a little crazy."

Eugene smiled, then he laughed. Then Paige laughed. It was more than a little crazy.

"What if we can't find him and all this has been a waste." She sobbed.

"No time spent with you is a waste," he smiled. "We just have to keep at it, we will find him. What happens then, I'm not one hundred percent sure , but I'm hoping we will know when we get there."

***

Wim slammed the taller thinner young man up against the wall hard. He was probably pushing it for his age but he was frustrated beyond recognition.

"On the ground," he screamed turning to the other two young Sudanese men in the corner.

They were not the problem. This guy, he had in a hold, had a machete on his belt and a look in his eye that said he would use it on Wim in a heartbeat. It had been an enquiry, not an operation. The young officer had just joined him on the gangland investigation and was following up a minor lead. There should have been no problems. Now the officer was knocked out on the floor and Wim was in a one against three. Wim pulled his cuffs out and managed to get one hand locked in. He pushed his right leg between the young mans legs and twisted hard on the young mans torso to pull his left side around without allowing his to expose and reach for the machete. Wim had completed this maneuver in real operations a lot, but he had spent a few years sitting behind a desk since the last time he needed it or practised it, so his old body creaked a little. The young man tried to squirm so Wim added a large smack over the back of the head with his fist clenched.

"Don't you even think about moving," he screamed again at the other two.

They were boys, but Wim's experience told him none of them could be underestimated. While the machete carrying suspect was still a little groggy he completed fixing the handcuffs and propped the boy down on his knees.

"OK, both of you, on your knees like this guy," he screamed again.

Wim reached down to get the handcuffs from the limp body of his junior detective and quickly applied them to the first of the boys in front of him. He expertly assessed the area and turned to strip an electrical cable from speaker that was on the desk nearby.

Just one moment he took his eye off the unbound boy and he was gone. Wim didn't even bother to chase, he knew he had no chance. Instead he grabbed his radio from his belt.

"Office329 reporting officer down, industrial estate building 427 left quadrant. Routine investigation gone sour. I repeat officer down in need of urgent medical. Remaining lone officer in need of backup."

"Roger 329. Units dispatched."

"Two suspects apprehended but a third suspect has fled on foot. Suspect is a Sudanese Male approximately 16 years old, tall and skinny wearing a black jacket, orange t-shirt and faded skinny jeans."

"Roger 329. Units dispatched to setup a perimeter around your location. Medical units expected ETA is three minutes."

Wim relaxed his grip on the radio. He had clenched to hard, his hands red for the strain. One of the bound boys tried to get up so Wim kicked him in the knees sending him tumbling to the floor.

"That may not have been textbook but it was satisfying," he shouted.

Wim turned to the junior officer.

"Dirk," he said in a loud voice. "Dirk, wake up, get up."

The junior officer didn't move. He checked Dirk's pulse and found it weak but present. He was happy when the ambulance arrived first with a squad car close behind allowing Wim to be free to take a breath.

The junior office, Dirk, was put into the back of the Ambulance and the squad car took away the offenders, they even caught the fleeing offender. Lots of work to do back in the office but Wim didn't want to waste this opportunity. This warehouse was known as a storehouse for gangland stolen cars and stolen goods. They would sit here, or in the yard and be distributed around Rotterdam by others. Generally they would only sit here for a few hours, less if the pickup could be secured earlier.

The desk in the corner had a few manifests and Wim took a moment to scan the contents and collect them as evidence. He checked the drawers and found a map of the old harbour area of Rotterdam he noticed three clear red crosses on residences, one in particular attracting his gaze.

The dream bakery.

He hadn't had time to check in on that case. He had even had the junior detective working on that case seconded into his unit, so he assumed there was no movement.

Wim collected a few more papers and headed back to the station where he set about questioning the assailants, asking what the map was for.

At first they didn't say anything, so he used some less than subtle speech lubrication techniques.

Then they did.

"It's a place we are watching, just watching for the boss." The kid with machete had said to him. "In this one we are looking for the guy that lives there. Short guy, Australian guy. Been a fat waste of time for six months."

"Why are you looking for the guy." Wim asked.

"Apparently the boss wants him gone." The machete kid was still young, but Wim knew some kids that age that had killed multiple times already.

"What do you mean by gone. My information said they are both already gone, left Rotterdam." Wim said.

"Well, then I would say dead," said the youth with a sly smirk on his face.

Wim was surprised.

"Why does your boss want him dead. What did the guy do?" Wim asked again.

"The boss took some money from him, the guy just wants it back," the kid laughed.

Wim didn't laugh. Had he got it wrong about those two?

***

Later that week Wim followed up by checking in on Adrie Winters. She had woken up and had been discharged from hospital. Wim called on her himself while she was recovering at home.

"Lovely man," Adrie said, "why would you suspect Eugene of anything. I had been under a lot of pressure, my husband passed away very unexpectedly and I discovered he was having an affair."

She looked at Wim with that devastated woman look he never liked.

"We have had a search order out for him but he has skipped out of Rotterdam to we don't know where." Wim had always just seen that fact as guilt.

"So because he left after I had a stroke he is guilty of what?" she asked.

"At a minimum he dropped you off at the hospital. He should have called an ambulance," Wim protested.

"Ambulances can take hours," she reminded Wim. "He probably saved my life."

"So why didn't he stay and say who he was and follow the procedure."

"I don't know detective, the man is Australian and maybe he just didn't know or maybe he had other things to do." Adrie was determined to be Eugene's greatest defender.

"At a maximum we have suspicions he caused your stroke and the death of another man. His name was Lem Forth, do you know him?" Wim was beginning to question his own logic.

"No pet," Adrie replied. "Did he die in the Dream Bakery?" she asked.

"No," Wim replied.

"Well. I don't know what you have but I just can't imagine Eugene doing anything like that." She was fairly adamant.

"OK. Thank you. I hope you are feeling better. If you remember anything else please contact me." Wim said pointing again to the card he had given Adrie earlier.

Wim walked to his car.

He was pretty sure, especially given his other work load that he would ask the Captain to drop this one. He had spoken to a number of the subjects from the dream bakery and they all backed Eugene in this way. Even if he had some hard proof of any crimes, which he didn't, he would struggle to get anyone in legal to prosecute. He had other things to get on with.

***

Eugene powered the Meteor over the crest and leaned into the bank to smoothly work the motorcycle around the bend. Paige hadn't done a lot of motorbike riding. Most had been on the back of scooters in Asia where there was no leaning and while they felt fast at the time, they weren't travelling this quick. Still Eugene had got them to the boat ramp everyday for a week safely, so she just held on and trusted him.

The morning was a bit hazy on the boat ramp, not its usual shining glory. The Viking 82 convertible sport-fishing yacht was way overkill for what they needed but Eugene liked to keep away from the crowds and it certainly achieved that. The vessel was fully equipped for prize fishing with a large viewing platform towering above the deck. It sprawled out in the front with a large white hull and had wood panelling around the main fishing chair in the back. Paige had chosen the largest of the five staterooms to spend time in. They didn't need such opulence but she did enjoy being able to take short trips around the Cayo Cordoba and Cayo Rocoso. The water was clear, the fish were amazing.

They had made the trip everyday that week but there was no old man. They had tried to see what the best time to go was, first based on the pictures in her dreams, then based on when most people went, then based on when most of the locals went. After a week they were no closer. They had been visiting a different restaurant everyday to ask, but no one knew. Juan, the boat captain, also had a few people on the lookout but they hadn't been successful either.

Even Paige's dreams had been letting her down. Well, truth was they were very nice. Relaxed and calm, full of very positive images and creative goldmines. She had been painting regularly and with Eugene at her side had found a kind of serenity she had never experienced before, especially now she had talked things out with her parents and her sister.

Today they had decided to try one of the seafood restaurants in the south of the island. On the other side from the villa they were staying. The seafood was great and the lady said she thought she knew the old man and that they could find him at Cedar Point.

The point was another ten minute ride from the restaurant, around the tip of the island. This part of the island was the least populated and was a beautiful picture with the sun setting in the west as they rode north towards the point.

Paige had the sun in her eyes but she could see someone sitting under a tree on a small wooden bench

"Eugene," she cried.

"I see him," Eugene replied riding the Meteor right up the bench.

The two of them took of there helmets. There in front of them was the old man. His eyes like hers, his nose like Eugene's.

"I have been waiting," he said.

The three of them sat and talked until the sun went down. They felt instantly comfortable like they knew each other.

***

The old man's name was Jose.

He lived in a small house walking distance from Cedar Point. His whole life had been spent on the island of San Andreas except one trip when he was a boy when his parents took him to New York City. He said it was a most profound trip, his father was injured by a stray bullet in a day time shooting of another man. His father had shown great bravery to protect he and his mother from the incident, but it cost him dearly and due to some long term complications of his injuries he passed before he was sixty. His mother lived another twenty four years with Jose taking on the role of carer for her as she aged.

He described his simple life in detail to them, first his time as a boy with his parents, his father a brilliant man, with great courage and a trendous apetite for learning and his mother an artist. He showed them some paintings his mother had done which adorned the living area of his family proudly. Jose's own life had been spent first as a farmer, then as a fisherman before taking an interest in local politics and becoming a state official which slowly became a more ceremonial role reminding those in power of the history of the island. In his later years Jose acted as a guide on the island, it was small but he was mostly known for his stories which he stored like winter wood and burned brightest when people would listen. Now, his age left him with little to do but some odd jobs around his family complex. Jose had a big family, but no children of his own he was a respected elder of his San Andres community but for the last few years had spent most of his time in this beautiful area around Cedar Point.

As darkness fell over the point two small girls came out to ask *Abuelo Jose* if he would be coming back to eat with the family tonight. Jose asked one girl to run back and tell her mother to set two extra places for his guests. He took the hand of the other girl as she led him back to the house.

The house was only small but full of life. The front had a large paved area where the family gathered, the house was a red brick design with a balcony that surrounded the perimeter to give relief from the tropical rains. It was simple but it met the needs of Jose, and the families of his brothers children. The courtyard was surrounded with flowers and tropical plants, the red brick pavement was so strinking in the overhead lights at night.

Paige was swept away by the ladies of the house as they all wanted to know who was Jose's new friends and how such strangers came to meet their *Abeulo.* Eugene sat and talked to Jose's nephews as they blended so well into this group from the other side of the world, like they had always been and they would always be, family.

***

Weeks had turned to months and months to years.

Eugene lay a wreath of flowers on the small memorial at Cedar Point and cleared the kerb set of leaves and debris. He stepped back, grasping Paige's hand as she wept.

"I miss him Eugene. He really completed us."

"He did," Eugene had to admit, Jose was an unlikely man of great intelligence and empathy. The world he lived in was so small but his understanding was so immense. In the short time they had together Eugene had learned so much, none of it written down but all of it profound.

"I would say he still does," Eugene said dipping down to look into the car seat cradle containing their son Julian.

"You can't say Julian doesn't have Jose's nose and eyes. A truly amazing piece of genetics as we have not one shared strand of DNA."

"That is your nose and they are my eyes," corrected Paige, picking up Julian from the cradle and touching his nose and eyes to confirm.

Julian looked up quietly.

"He does just seem to know," Paige said.

Chapter Eleven

All things must pass

Paige held Julian's hand tight as they stood at the front of the room. She didn't have the courage to speak, so she left the talking to him.

"It was his time. If he could say it, he would say. All things must pass."

Julian had spoken so confidently and lovingly for over twenty minutes now, somehow maintaining the strength to tell the small gathering of people in the Sunshine Funeral Home, the highlights of his father's life.

Paige had closed her eyes briefly. She knew it was true and she leaned heavily on Julian, the part of Eugene that she could still hold. She could see in him so much of Eugene. Not just his father's nose, Julian had his fathers keen mind and kind hands. Emblazoned on his brow was his fathers intelligence and strapped to his chest his father courage in himself. Julian was a man who achieved so much and thirsted for more, but today was shrouded in reflection.

"The essence of this small statement wraps up my father. Intelligent, thoughtful, unconventional but above all pragmatic. His life was a journey, the objective of which was not always clear to those around him and certainly not something he would share, unless success was imminent or already achieved."

A brief laughter fell across the room. Eugene did indeed keep his own counsel.

"Above all he showed respect and kindness to us all. He asked, when he could have taken. Gave, when he could have walked away and fostered empathy and compassion in his mutual support of this and the global community."

Paige's tears flowed again. Her son had such a way with words.

"Let's not forget his pursuit, his quest, his dream for our dreams." Julian paused a moment. Paige wasn't sure but she though, surprisingly, he was collecting his nerve. "His work in the field of Oneirology will form the basis for further research for the next hundred years. His philanthropic support of dream understanding, mutual dreaming, lucid dreaming, recurring dreams, dream videography and biographical dreaming has given rise to a community that has produced insightful and practical solutions for us all."

"So here today, we mourn the man, none more than Mum and I, while the world mourns the loss of a titan in his field. I am sure he would be first to want us to not linger, to put that behind us and look to the future."

Paige's hand shook as Julian led her back to her seat. Her eyes, hollow and red, she hid behind her favourite sunglasses. She couldn't see how she could make it through the rest of the day. The energy she had expended to this point was beyond what she could muster. Just one more song.

Eugene had picked the music to play. When Julian went through the list with her there were a few songs she couldn't recall so the two of them spent some time yesterday listening.

She had cried, the choices were very Eugene. But this final one she just didn't understand. It was by an Australian artist Missy Higgins, called "Forgive Me."

The guitar started slowly lulling her to think the song would affect her differently this time. Because she had heard it before.

But the first line gripped her.

"Oh, my son. Look at what I've done. But I am learning still, learning still, know that I am learning still."

Paige's tears ran down her face freely.

He had no grounds to need forgiveness. That would assume he had done something wrong. But that was Eugene's way, somewhere in his moral compass.

"Oh my wife, you are my life, I am burning still, burning still, know that I am burning for you still."

Whatever it was that he saw, she had forgiven.

***

Paige woke abruptly.

A small girl had sat next to her, comforted her and beckoned her.

She should let it go. Dreams were just dreams, right.

But the girl had his nose.